TAKESHITA
DEMONS

To adventurous children everywhere, with monster-loads of thanks to my family – C.B

The publishers and the author would like to thank Mrs Keiko Holt
for checking the Japanese language and traditions

JANETTA OTTER-BARRY BOOKS

First published in Great Britain in 2010 by
Frances Lincoln Children's Books, 4 Torriano Mews,
Torriano Avenue, London NW5 2RZ
www.franceslincoln.com

First hardback edition published in the USA in 2010

A catalogue record for this book is available from the British Library.

ISBN 978-1-84780-143-2

Set in Palatino

Printed in Singapore by KHL Printing Co. Pte Ltd. in July 2010

1 3 5 7 9 8 6 4 2

TAKESHITA
DEMONS

CRISTY BURNE

ILLUSTRATED BY SIKU

F

FRANCES LINCOLN
CHILDREN'S BOOKS

CHAPTER ONE

Are you afraid of ghosts and evil spirits, or the black space under your bed? If you are, then put this book down right away and choose another. If I were you, I would choose a book about teddy bears and bunny rabbits, because then there's a good chance that you won't be reading about floating heads or evil spirits or any of the other things you'll find inside this book. If I were you, I'd do that. But for me, it's already too late.

I was born in a small town near Osaka, in Japan. My family moved to England just over a year ago, after my grandmother died. But our troubles started long before that. Looking back, I should have realised earlier.

My father worked long hours for his office job, so he didn't realise either. He was never at home to see what was happening. My brother Kazu was too little even to notice; he was still a baby back then. And my mother was always busy with Kazu or her English class, plus she didn't really believe. That just left my grandmother, Baba. She understood better than all of them.

Baba knew all there was to know about spirits and demons, good and evil, and she took care to protect our family from them. She kept a cedar leaf over our front door to ward off evil, she always left toys and games out for our house ghost, she even kept a pair of shiisa lion-dogs on the mantelpiece, bought during a beach holiday to Okinawa when my dad was just a boy. She never got sick or forgetful or even caught a cold, not in the whole time I'd known her, which was all my life. But towards the end, when she got really old, she walked with a stick and her hands shook like leaves whenever she used her chopsticks. She died when I was only eleven.

I cried and cried at her funeral, I didn't care who saw me. People from all over Kawanishi sent in envelopes of money and wreaths of flowers. The entire room was filled with light, and the priest was ringing his bell to keep out the bad spirits and bid farewell to my grandmother on her journey to her new place. Afterwards my family served a feast

6

of noodles and tempura upstairs, but nobody ate. Instead the rows of guests, all dressed in black, just knelt on the tatami mats and made smalltalk about the seasons. The noodles went cold and the tempura went soggy. Baba would have thought it an awful waste.

But what does all this have to do with floating heads and evil spirits? I didn't know myself, not back then. But Baba knew. So just remember: it's not too late to close this book and read about something safe instead, like teddy bears and bunny rabbits. Don't say I didn't warn you.

Until we moved to London I'd lived in the same house all my life, the same house Baba had lived in when she was just a girl. It was the oldest house in our street, wooden and two stories high. Its floors were polished smooth from generations of feet, and you could skid the entire length of the hallway if you got up enough speed in your socks. It creaked in the wind and was cold in the night, but it hid a thousand secrets, most of which my Baba knew. The biggest secret was our sakabashira pillar.

That was the reason we had a house ghost watching over us, the reason that nothing horrible had ever happened to our family. Not yet.

A sakabashira pillar is basically a mix-up. Ours happened more than a hundred years ago, when the men who were building our living room accidentally stuck the top end of a huge wooden column into the ground, so that its bottom end was pointing at the roof. It didn't change the shape of our house, and we couldn't tell that the pillar was upside-down, but none of that mattered. The damage was done. Our house was doomed to be haunted.

You can never tell what sort of ghost a sakabashira pillar will attract. Luckily, my Baba's Baba was as wise as my Baba; she managed to attract the attention of a zashiki-warashi, a child-ghost. Ours was a little girl, about five years old, and Baba called her Zashiko. I never saw her, but sometimes I'd wake in the night to find my pillow down by my feet instead of under my head. Other times I'd wake to see the light above me swaying in the ceiling, silent and watching, gently rocking, like a swing. But I was never scared. Being haunted by Zashiko was the best thing that could have happened to our family. She played tricks, but she also brought good luck and kept us safe from the other spirits and demons, the ones Baba always warned me about.

When we left our house, we left Zashiko behind. With Baba gone and Zashiko back in Japan, we were truly alone when we arrived in England. I thought we'd be safe, that the spirits wouldn't find us. I was wrong.

Chapter Two

The woman knocked on our apartment door just before dinner on Monday night.

"Miku, can you get that?" Mum called from the kitchen.

I don't know why she even asked. Dad wasn't home yet and it wasn't as if Kazu could get it. He couldn't even reach the door handle.

I should have been studying for a maths test, but all those numbers and equations were doing my head in. I was glad for any interruption. Perhaps it was Dad, back early but forgotten his keys. Or it might be our neighbour, the cute one with the noisy scooter that Mum always complained about.

"Miku?" Mum called again.

"I'm going," I said, getting up from the table and heading down the hall.

I was only a few paces from the door when a strange feeling came over me. Baba had always taught me to be careful about opening our front door, and this time especially, I knew she was right.

"Who is it?" I asked, speaking through the wood.

"Red Cross," a woman's sweet voice replied.

It wasn't Dad or our cute neighbour. It was a stranger. She sounded OK. Certainly no maniac kidnapper, like Mum was always warning about. But how did she get into the building?

I rested my hand on the door handle, ready to open the door. But then I stopped. Something wasn't right. I could feel it.

"Red Cross," the woman's voice repeated, a little muffled through the door. "Would you like to make a donation?"

I'd seen Mum make donations before, for the Salvation Army and the RSPCA, but something about this woman's voice was making me feel strange. I wished I could see through the little peephole in our door, but it was too high up, and I'd left it too late to drag over a chair.

"Red Cross," the woman's voice said. "Red Cross. Would you like to make a donation?"

Still I hesitated. Was something wrong here?

I didn't know what to do.

The door sounded again.

Knock... Knock... Knock...

"Red Cross," the woman droned. "Would you like to make a donation?"

She was beginning to freak me out. I took a step away from the door.

"Miku," Mum called from the kitchen, sounding annoyed. "Could you please get the door?"

But I didn't yell back an answer. I was already backing away from the door. My stomach was starting to fold in on itself. Something was very wrong.

"Red Cross," the voice said. "Would you like to make a donation?"

Knock... Knock...

"Red Cross. Would you like to make a donation?"

I kept backing away from the voice, keeping my eyes on the door handle, watching for a sign.

Suddenly I bumped into something behind me. I gasped, nearly swallowing my tongue.

"Miku."

"Mum..."

"*Nani shiteruno, Miku?* What are you doing?" she complained. "Couldn't you at least get the door?" She had a tea towel over one shoulder and Kazu

on one hip. She did not look happy. Kazu didn't seem to notice. He was smiling and trying to stick a partly chewed carrot stick in her ear.

"But Mum..."

I had to explain. Stop her. Do something.

"Who is it?" Mum asked through the door.

"Red Cross," the woman's voice replied. "Would you like to make a donation?"

"But Mum…"

I tried to get between her and the door, to tell her that something was very wrong with whatever was waiting outside.

But Mum just looked at me and sighed, then she turned the handle.

I was too late.

The door swung open. A gust of frozen air came sweeping into the house. It felt like a wind straight from the arctic. Kazu's soft black hair flared up as if someone had blown a hairdryer in his face. But there was no one in the hallway. The entire area was empty.

"Hello?" Mum asked, poking her head out of the door to check the vacant hallway.

There was nobody there.

"Really, Miku," Mum grumbled, pulling the door shut with a bang. "That poor woman. She probably got tired of waiting and now she's outside in the cold. *Kondo wa ne*. Next time..." She didn't need to finish her sentence. She just looked at me as if I was a failed cooking project. Kazu seemed to agree. He threw his carrot stick on the floor, whimpering.

Mum turned the door lock into place. Her silence meant disapproval. But how could I explain? I grabbed Kazu's slimy carrot stick from the floor.

"Mum," I began. "I think that woman was..." What? An evil spirit? A demon? Mum didn't believe all the stuff Baba had taught me. She didn't even believe in placing a cedar leaf over the door.

The cedar leaf! My heart sank. Surely not.

"Mum, did you move the cedar leaf?"

Mum looked away. "Not now, Miku," she said, moving back down the hall to the kitchen, Kazu still on one hip. He coughed a little and then started crying.

I followed them into the kitchen, dumping the slimed carrot in the bin. This was urgent. "The cedar leaf. The one over the front door. Did you move it?"

Kazu coughed again and then started screaming like the fire alarm at school. Mum ignored my question, jiggling him up and down on her hip, then sitting down with him on a kitchen chair.

"Shhhh," she crooned, still bouncing him on her lap. "You're OK, Kazu-chan, you're all right."

But I had an awful feeling my brother wasn't OK at all.

I raced back to the front door, dragging a chair over so I could search the top of the door frame with my fingertips. I had a whole shoebox of cedar leaves under my bed. I'd brought them all the way from Kawanishi to London, pretending it was a shoebox of calligraphy paper so Mum wouldn't take them off me. For nearly a year I'd worked to keep a cedar leaf stuck over our front door at all times, replacing the leaves that Mum would sweep or dust away. But this time my fingers came up bare. I hadn't replaced this one fast enough. And now it was too late.

I'd never seen an amazake-baba. I'd heard my own Baba speak of them many times. They were old women, with honey-sweet voices. She said they came knocking on your door late at night, bringing illness and disease to all who answered. But there was, of course, one easy way to keep amazake-baba away. A cedar leaf, stuck over the front door. But we hadn't had a leaf stuck there tonight.

From the kitchen I could hear Kazu still coughing. Coughing. Crying. I kept remembering the cold wind that had blown into our house when Mum had opened the door. The way Kazu's hair had shifted in the breeze. All that my Baba had told me. I stuck a new cedar leaf over our door, but I knew the damage had already been done.

Kazu coughed all night, keeping Mum awake with worry so her eyes looked tired and bruised the next morning. And he coughed all through breakfast, his little face red with the effort.

"I'm taking him to the doctor," Mum announced, not touching her morning rice. "He's not getting any better."

Dad nodded, slurping coffee as he looked through his paper. "*So da ne* – I agree," he said, looking up briefly. "You better try for an early appointment. The forecast's not good. They're predicting snow."

It was the first sign that bad things were coming our way. The spirits had discovered us. And they'd found a way in.

CHAPTER THREE

I nearly froze as soon as I stepped outside our door on Tuesday morning. The wind was blowing and it was starting to sleet. By the time I got to school my shoes and socks were soaked through. My feet and fingers felt like blocks of ice. And worse, when I walked into class, everyone turned to stare at me. I probably looked like a drowned cat. But I soon figured out they weren't staring at that.

Alex opened his big mouth first, pointing from me to the front of the class. Instead of Mr Lloyd, there was a tall, dark-haired woman writing on the board. The whole class stank of sickly sweet jasmine, as if she'd had some sort of accident with her perfume bottle.

"Is she your mum?" Alex asked.

The woman was dressed up as if she was about

to read the news on TV. She was wearing a shiny caramel skirt with a white blouse and matching caramel jacket. Her hair was long and black and just as shiny as her skirt, and she wore it tied around her head like an elaborate piece of origami. She had her back to the class and was writing something on the board with purple chalk. It was hard to read, but I could just make out the letters:

MRS OKUDA

"Well, is she?" Alex asked again.

I walked past him to the desk that Cait and I shared. Her seat was still empty and there was no sign of her bag. Unlucky. I could usually count on Cait to back me up when Alex was being an idiot.

"No," I answered. "Is she *your* mum?"

I pulled my pencil case and books out of my favourite bag and began setting up my desk for the day.

"She looks like your mum," Alex hissed. He had turned around in his seat so he could talk to me more easily.

"She's not my mum," I said. I focused on my books, wishing Alex would shut up. It was as if he'd never seen someone from Japan before. I wasn't the only Japanese person in the world.

"She your aunt then?"

Great. This was going to be tedious. But just as Alex was getting started, the strange toffee-suited teacher spoke.

"Good morning, class," she began.

Alex turned to face the front almost immediately, leaving me blissfully alone. This woman, whoever she was, had saved me! For a moment I thought I might even like her, despite her awful outfit and smelly perfume and enormous hair. But I was wrong.

"My name is Mrs Okuda. Mr Lloyd has fallen ill and I will be teaching your class while he is away." The woman smiled, revealing two rows of sparkling white teeth surrounded by glowing purple lipstick.

A ripple passed across the class. I guess they were staring at the same thing as me. Her lipstick and stinky perfume were bad enough, but the rest of her was worse. Her whole face was caked in pale make-up and the white collar of her blouse rode high across her neck, like something from those old-fashioned movies where the women all wear petticoats and need maids to help them dress. She also wore several strings of tight white pearls, crammed across her throat. It looked as if her head might fall off at any moment, cut off at the neck from lack of oxygen. It was the worst outfit I'd ever seen on a teacher.

Someone giggled and I saw Alex whisper to his neighbour. We all knew what a supply teacher meant, especially a woman teacher, and especially one dressed as badly as this. It meant watching videos, no maths test, heaps of free time, and the chance to make her really, really angry without getting into too much trouble. I bounced my freezing feet under the desk, wondering what Alex would do to get it started.

"So," Mrs Okuda continued, oblivious to the whispers and nudges of the class. "Let's get to know each other better, shall we?" She smiled again, baring her teeth like a fox, this time directly at me. I looked down at once, examining the grooves in the wood of my desk. Just because we had the same coloured hair and the same kind of skin it didn't mean I needed special attention. I'd kind of hoped she wouldn't notice I was Japanese. She'd be better off keeping her eye on Alex.

"Shall we start by calling the roll?" she asked, but she didn't wait for an answer. She pulled out a brown folder of papers and took the lid off a black pen. "Oscar? Jean? Imran?"

A high-pitched screech echoed from outside, in the corridor. With a squeal of web rubber, Cait came bursting in through the door, her umbrella dripping with ice and her hair still rammed in a woolly hat. "Sorry, Mr Llo..." she began, then stopped in her tracks, staring at Mrs Okuda.

Mrs Okuda stopped her roll call to glance at Cait, who must have been making a large puddle in the doorway. "You can leave your umbrella outside," she said. "And you are?"

"Cait O'Neill," said Cait, and she glanced across the class, smiling a quick hello at me.

"Right, thank you, Cait," Mrs Okuda said, scanning her roll and making a mark with her pen. "You may sit. Don't be late again." Then she continued with the roll call.

Cait dropped her umbrella outside and came to take her seat next to me. I didn't look across. I had a feeling something bad was going to happen.

"Alex. Shaun. Isabella."

She was getting close. I could hear my heart beating louder.

"Jackson? Robyn? Ursula?"

Then it happened. When she got to my name, Mrs Okuda stopped, smiling her awful smile right at me. "Takeshita Miku," she said, saying my full name, with the family name first, the proper Japanese way.

I cringed. "Yes," I answered, wishing she'd

treat me just like all the other kids. "But it's Miku..."
I dared to correct her, glaring as Alex turned around.

"Miku Mouse," Alex mouthed silently, mocking my name.

But Mrs Okuda didn't seem to notice. Instead, even worse, she spoke to me in Japanese.

"*Anata mo Nihonjin desu-ne*? You are also Japanese, aren't you?" she said, as if it wasn't obvious from my name already.

Heat rose from my collar in waves. This had never happened before. I could feel the other kids turning round in their seats, staring. I never spoke Japanese at school. Why was she doing this?

"Yes, Miss," I answered in English. I stared at my desk, willing her to stop. It had been bad enough when I was new at school. I did not need this now.

"*Kyou wa samukunai*?" she continued, as if she was completely oblivious to the shame she was causing me.

Talk English, I wanted to scream. What are you doing? Instead I answered politely, hoping she'd think enough was enough and get on with the roll call. "Yes, Miss, quite cold today." What was she doing, asking me about the weather? In Japan it was normal for strangers to talk about the weather. In England too I'd noticed, but she didn't need to do it in front of the whole class. Please.

But still she didn't stop.

"Mada Nihongo wo hanasu yo ne. So you still speak Japanese." She narrowed her eyes. "And I guess you still know...."

I couldn't look, I just sank lower in my chair. She hadn't asked a direct question, so I figured she didn't want a direct answer. I decided to stay silent. And there had been something strange in the way she'd spoken. As if she wasn't even speaking to me, but to herself, somewhere in the back of her shiny trussed-up head. And what did she mean by "still know"?

I could hear the clock ticking, could feel every pair of eyes in the room focused on me, burning holes of shame into the top of my skull. I willed Mrs Okuda to forget about me and start calling the roll again.

Then, thankfully, something broke the silence. It wasn't Mrs Okuda finishing the roll. She'd missed heaps of kids' names out, but it was as if she'd forgotten all about roll call. Instead, she was writing something on the board. The chalk screeched, and slowly chairs rumbled as the other kids turned to face the front. I steamed with relief.

When the chalk squeaked to a stop, I sneaked a look at the board.

ABOUT ME, read the ghastly purple chalk.

"An essay," Mrs Okuda announced. "Write me an essay, introducing yourself. It should be two pages long, no pictures. Due lunchtime. Any questions?"

The class groaned. Alex's hand shot high in the air.

"Yes?" Mrs Okuda asked, flashing her white and purple smile.

"On Tuesday mornings we play dodgeball in the gym," Alex smirked.

"Yes?" she asked, waiting.

"Well, we won't have time to do essays before lunch if we're playing dodgeball."

"Then we'll have to give dodgeball a miss for today." Mrs Okuda smiled, then she sat at Mr Lloyd's desk, crossing her legs as if that closed the conversation.

Other kids' hands went up almost at once.

"Yes?" she asked, sounding slightly annoyed.

"When will Mr Lloyd be back?" someone asked.

"I don't know. He's quite sick."

"What kind of sick?"

"Hands in the air," Mrs Okuda said, but she answered anyway. "He has chicken pox." She smiled. "It can be quite severe in adults. It could be several weeks before he gets back." She looked across at me, making eye contact before I could snatch my eyes away. She looked pleased and her eyes were shining.

No one else seemed to share her enthusiasm. Several weeks? No dodgeball? For seconds there was a stand-off. No one moved. No one spoke. We just sat there, looking at Mrs Okuda, who just sat there, looking back. She seemed as hard and shiny as a toffee.

Then Alex broke the silence, putting up his hand.

"Can I go to the toilet? I'm busting."

"Me too," said Oscar, his desk partner, waving his hand in the air.

"I feel sick," said another kid, his hand shooting up. "I think I might puke."

"I'm gonna pee right now," Alex added, wriggling. "Miss, I can't hold it in."

A few kids giggled from near the door, but Mrs Okuda didn't seem to hear them. She didn't move at all. Instead she seemed to grow taller, as if she were somehow stretching up and over Mr Lloyd's desk. In seconds she seemed to be hanging over the whole class, even though she was still sitting down.

Her voice boomed down, slow and calm. "You will work," she said. "And you will work quietly. There will be no trouble from this class."

Everyone fell silent, even Alex. Hands went down, kids stopped wriggling, feet stopped kicking the desk in front. One by one, the class opened their desks and pulled out paper and pens.

Mrs Okuda knew she'd won. "Two pages," she said. "Before lunch. I will answer any legitimate questions."

The class began writing with hardly a whisper. Even Alex. I could hear the clock ticking. We were never this quiet for a supply teacher, not even for Mr Lloyd. A girl near the front put up her hand and Mrs Okuda went to help her with her question.

I glanced across at Cait, who was trying to take things out of her bag without making too much noise.

"What happened to you?" I whispered.

"Bus," she replied. "The weather..." Cait's family lived right on the outskirts of the catchment area for our school. She had to travel by bus every morning, but some afternoons she came back to mine till her dad could pick her up after his work. "Where'd she come from?" Cait asked, pointing at Mrs Okuda.

"Dunno." I rolled my eyes. We'd never had a supply teacher quite like her before. I opened my notebook at a blank page and took the lid off a pen.

"Okuda," Cait said. "Is that Japanese?"

"Yep," I nodded. I didn't mind if Cait asked me about being Japanese. She'd been round to our flat often enough to see what it was like. Plus she was Irish and had mad curly hair, so she knew what it was like to be different. "She was speaking Japanese earlier."

"I thought so. Strange. Maybe she just wanted to be friendly?"

I raised an eyebrow. Since when did I want to get friendly with a teacher?

Cait grinned at me. "Don't worry. Hey, can I come to yours this afternoon? My dad'll pick me up before tea."

"Sure..."

"Takeshita-san." Mrs Okuda's voice snapped like a whip from the front of the class. She was looking up at me from where she stood helping the girl, still using my surname instead of my real name. "*Shizuka-ni*," she commanded. Silence.

Embarrassment steamed off me. Would she insist on doing this all day? All week? Cait put her head down and began writing her essay. I knew I should start writing mine, but there was nothing I wanted to say. Nothing I wanted to tell this woman about myself. I didn't want her to know anything at all ABOUT ME.

I heard her move to help another kid up the front, so I sneaked another look. Her hair was so shiny it seemed fake, like a wig or a costume. And her jacket was way too tight. She looked like a badly dressed skeleton, not a teacher. Why couldn't we have Mr Lloyd back? I almost missed him. He wore funny cardigans with awful turtleneck sweaters, but he never...

And then my heart froze. My breath stopped. I'd seen something. Something no one else would understand. I nearly choked with the shock.

But perhaps there was some mistake? I took a slow breath and tried to calm down. Perhaps I hadn't seen what I thought I'd seen? I had to look again, but when I did, there was no denying it.

Mrs Okuda was itching at her neck. She was digging her painted fingers deep down beneath her collar and through her crowded pearls, as if to scratch a violent itch. But that wasn't the bad bit. As she dug, I'd seen a flash of red through the white. It had been ink red, usually a colour of protection, but not in this case. This red took the form of tiny Japanese characters, tattooed like old blood into the skin of her throat. I couldn't read them, they were too small and she was too far away. But I didn't need to read them. I already knew what they meant.

Hand shaking, I took a deep breath and tried to stay focused on my pencil, on the blank page. But already my mind was racing. It was as my Baba had told me in her most horrible stories. Mrs Okuda was a nukekubi, or a 'cut-throat' in English. A demon. A type I'd never seen before.

But what was she doing in London? And why was she teaching my class?

CHAPTER FOUR

I handed in my two-page essay just before lunch, like all the rest of the class, but I made sure it was a complete load of make-believe. I pretended to love chess and football, flower arranging and cake baking: all things I totally hate. But right then I would have played ten games of football and baked a dozen cakes. Anything to keep the nukekubi off my scent. Thanks to my Baba, I knew exactly what I was dealing with.

Baba had told me all about their kind. By day they seemed like ordinary people, except for the red symbols around their neck. Those symbols were like the teeth of a zipper: they marked the place where the nukekubi's head would come flying off. As soon as it was dark, when its body was safely hidden away, the nukekubi would go hunting. I'd seen pictures of nukekubi, and Baba had told me stories that would make your toes curl up at night in fear. About children who disappeared from their beds, never to be seen again. About dogs and goats that went missing in the night, their clean bones discovered the next day. Once (and this was never proved, but Baba believed it to be true), a nukekubi ate an entire classroom of kids on their Second Year school camp. One night the cabins were full of boys and girls, laughing and telling ghost stories. The next morning, there was nothing left but their futons. Not even their bones were found.

The thing is, nukekubi can do more than just send their heads flying around like mini aeroplanes, zipping through windows, down chimneys, round corners and into your house. Nukekubi are hunters. Meat-eaters. While their bodies are safely sleeping in bed, their heads can detach and zoom about, sniffing around for a tasty meal. Children are their favourite. Puppies and kittens come next. But according to Baba, they weren't fussy. They'd eat anything that was young and fresh and tasty.

"Takeshita-san…"

The sound of Mrs Okuda's singsong voice was like sandpaper in my ears. Each time she opened her purple-lipped mouth I expected to see it come zooming towards me, sharp teeth bared. Each time I felt like running away, screaming for my Baba to save me.

But that wasn't an option. I was trapped in a classroom with all the other kids. I couldn't just run home and call the police. What would I say? Excuse me, but this woman's head is probably going to fly off and eat me once the sun goes down tonight. No. I didn't think so.

"Takeshita-san." She wouldn't leave me alone. "Would you like to read your essay to the class?" she asked, teeth shining. She was waving my essay pages in one long-fingered hand.

I looked down at my own hands, picking at a fingernail. I thought if I stayed silent she might leave me alone. Fat chance.

"Takeshita-san," she said. "Read your essay to the class." This was no longer a request. It was an order. The rest of the class sat silent. They'd hardly moved all morning. Even Alex hadn't teased me when Mrs Okuda kept using my surname.

"Erm." There was no way I was going up there to stand next to her. No way in the world.

But Mrs Okuda thought differently. "Takeshita-san," she said, narrowing her eyes and pursing her purple lips till they were thin and tight as veins. *"Sakubun yonde*. Read it." She snapped out the words, using Japanese so rude my mother would have slapped me. She held my essay out, her caramel arm pointing right at my head, as if she was a kyudo master lining me up in the sights of an invisible arrow.

The other kids sat still as statues. Not even Alex turned round. A strange quiet fell upon the classroom, as if we were waiting for something to explode. I hoped it would be Mrs Okuda. I held my breath and watched as colour flooded her face. She was flushing almost as purple as her lipstick. What would happen next? Could her head fly off, right in the middle the day?

"Takeshita-san." She was hissing now. She took a step forward and my heart started knocking so hard I could hear it banging against the wood of my desk. Perhaps her head would come flying off and eat me right there and then.

At that moment there was a brisk tap at the door.

Mrs Okuda froze, her arm still outstretched, pointing.

The door swung open and our deputy head, Mrs Thompson, came trotting in.

She was dressed in plain black trousers with a neat blue jumper, and she didn't look a bit as if she was going to send her head flying round the room to eat me. I could have kissed her.

"Morning, Mrs..." Mrs Thompson paused, obviously unsure of our supply teacher's name.

"Okuda," mouthed our shiny teacher, the colour draining from her face. "Mrs Okuda." She quickly pulled her pointing hand back down to her side.

"Mrs Okuda." Mrs Thompson beamed at her. "Morning, class." She smiled at us. "I trust you've been behaving for Mrs Okuda?" She took a quick glance at Alex's desk and seemed satisfied with what she saw. He was sitting quietly for a change.

"Can I help you, Mrs Thompson?" Mrs Okuda asked, recovering her composure. She tried to match Mrs Thompson's smile, baring her purple-rimmed teeth. She looked more like a wolf.

"I've come with dreadful news," Mrs Thompson said, smiling. She looked as if her news was about as dreadful as winning a year's supply of free ice-cream or getting all the numbers in the Jackpot Lotto.

"Yes...?" Mrs Okuda leaned in, eager to hear more.

I held my breath. Did Mrs Thompson know about the nukekubi? Was she sending the police? Was my little brother OK?

Mrs Thompson looked around the class, enjoying her moment in the spotlight.

"Yes?" Mrs Okuda asked again.

"You've all got the rest of the day off school," Mrs Thompson announced at last, throwing her arms wide as if she was presenting prizes at assembly. "It's snowing outside and the forecast is for more snow. You should all make your way home early, before lunch. It looks as if the roads and footpaths might soon be snowed over."

A massive weight lifted from the class. Kids started chatting with their neighbours or packing their bags in a rush. I didn't wait to hear more. I packed my bag just as fast as the rest of them. It was time to get out.

Mrs Thompson filled us in on sensible snow-related details. We were to go straight home, no dilly-dallying. If the snow was still bad in the morning, we were to ring the school and ask for advice about whether to come in. And under no circumstances were we to make the journey into school tomorrow if it was in any way dangerous or icy.

Her words washed over me like a dream. I didn't care about the snow. All I wanted was to get as far away from Mrs Okuda as I could, somewhere safe.

I needed to think of a plan. We had to get rid of her.

Minutes later, with the caramel Okuda monster watching us in silence from the front of the class, we said goodbye to Mrs Thompson, collected our coats and left. I didn't wait to see which of us was last to leave the class. I just grabbed Cait and we scooted out fast enough to leave burn marks in the carpet.

I could feel Mrs Okuda's eyes on my back as we left.

But I didn't turn round, and we didn't stop to say goodbye.

Chapter Five

Mrs Thompson had been right. The snow was coming down in big flakes and it was already thick on the ground.

"Awesome." Cait kicked a puff of fresh white snow into the air. "I can't believe we get to go home early. And we missed the maths test. Just awesome. Is it still OK if I come to yours? 'Cos my dad'll still be at work and all. Hey, isn't this amazing?" She dusted some flakes off her jacket and kicked up another cloud of snow. "Do you want to make a mini snowman?"

"We've got to get home." I pulled on her arm. We had no time for snowmen, mini or otherwise. "Didn't you see that woman back there? Mrs Okuda?"

"Oh yeah," Cait said, kicking her feet through the snow and almost keeping up with me as

I barrelled ahead. She didn't seem too worried. "You were great. I can't believe she kept calling you Takeshita-san. And talking all that Japanese? You were right to ignore her. I wouldn't have read out my essay either."

The snow kept falling. It seemed even heavier when we turned into my street. Lucky we didn't have far to go. Usually it was a bit awkward, living so close to school. Almost every day I'd accidentally run into other kids, or even worse, a teacher. Usually I'd be doing something totally uncool, like buying nappies for Kazu or heading to the shops with my mum. But today, living right next to school was the best thing that could have happened. We'd soon be inside, and safe.

"I'm not talking about the essay," I said. "I'm talking about her. Okuda. Her neck. Didn't you see?"

"See what? Oh, that. Totally. That was the worst outfit I've ever seen. Who did she think she was? I can't believe we have to have her till Mr Lloyd gets back. Wonder what she'll wear tomorrow?"

"No!" I fumbled with my key, trying to get in as quickly as possible, without my fingers freezing off or a flying head coming to chew on my ears. "Her neck. The marks? Didn't you notice her itching?"

The door opened and we stepped inside the hallway of our building. I shut the door behind us, banging it hard so the lock clicked into place. Then I leaned back against the door and looked across at Cait. She looked fed up with all my questions. And no wonder. I was being an awful best friend.

"I'm sorry," I said.

Cait kicked the snow off her shoes. "S'ok. Just tell me what you're going on about."

"Come on," I said, grabbing her arm. "Come upstairs. I'll show you."

We rushed up the stairs to the door of our flat. I buzzed the doorbell and knocked twice for good measure.

Cait bent down to unlace her shoes. She'd been round often enough to know that we had a shoes-off policy for our home. Your toes sometimes got cold in winter, but we kept pairs of slippers at the door, even a special pair of guest slippers for Cait. They were moss green and had cartoon kittens on them, but Cait didn't seem to mind.

"So what's the big deal then?" she asked, her shoes loosened and ready to kick off. "Why the big fuss about Okuda's neck?"

"Did you see her marks?" I asked, indicating my own throat.

"No, I already told you."

I buzzed the door again. What was keeping Mum so long?

"Red marks," I said. "Little ones, kind of like mosquito bites, but all in a line."

"Oh, yeah. I did see something like that. I thought they were mozzy bites. She was itching a lot."

"Yes, that's it." Cait had seen them too! I could have hugged her, but just then the lock on our door clicked open.

"Hello?" said a voice behind the door, but it wasn't Mum's.

"Hello?" I echoed, stepping back as the door swung wider. Who was this? Where was Mum?

"Miku!" The voice sounded pleased. "What are you doing home so early? And it's Cait, isn't it? Come in, come in. You must be freezing." It was my neighbour, Mrs Williams, the one with the cute son and the noisy scooter. She looked a bit frazzled, with bits of brown hair sticking up out of place and no make-up. "I came as soon as I could. Your poor mother."

My poor mother? What was going on?

Cait and I kicked off our shoes and scuffed our way into a pair of slippers each.

"What about my mum? Where's Kazu?"

"He's right here, on the sofa," said Mrs Williams, walking ahead of us down the hall. "Still sick, the poor little blighter. I guess your mum will take him to the doctor's when she gets back."

"Gets back from where?" I asked. I rushed past Mrs Williams into the living room, scared of what I might find.

But I found Kazu sitting happily on the sofa, just like Mrs Williams had said. I tried to gather him in my arms, but he whinged and pushed me away, more interested in watching the TV. So that, at least, was normal.

"Your teacher didn't tell you?" Mrs Williams waddled into the living room with Cait following close behind.

"Tell me what?"

"I left a message with the school. They must've forgotten. Your mother's in the hospital, dear. She was putting out the rubbish and she slipped on some ice. It's been so unusually cold..."

The news made me shiver. "But..."

"Don't worry, dear." Mrs Williams patted me on the shoulder. "It's nothing too serious. She'll be

44

back tomorrow, I expect. She's asked me to look after Kazu till your father gets back."

Back tomorrow? But that could be too late! I realised I'd been counting on Mum. She might not believe in cedar leaves or amazaki-baba, but she couldn't just stand back and do nothing if I told her our supply teacher was a nukekubi. She would have to make a plan. She would know what to do. She was Japanese after all.

"Can I get you a cup of something warm, dears?" Mrs Williams asked, hovering while I scrubbed my hands together with anxiety and the cold.

What to do? We couldn't count on Mum. That meant we were alone till Dad got back. We were going to need a plan of our own.

"Um, no thanks," I said, thinking fast. "We've got homework. They sent us home early cos of the snow, but we've still got heaps of work."

"Ah." Mrs Williams looked relieved. I guess she wanted to hang out with us about as much as we wanted to hang out with her. "Well, have fun. I'll let you know when your father calls."

I nodded. Cait and I zoomed up the stairs as fast as our slippers would climb, heading straight for my bedroom. We burst through the door and I made sure to close it behind us.

"What?" Cait had run out of patience. She sat down and glared at me. "I don't want to do homework. Will you just tell me what's going on?"

At last we were safe, and alone. I sat cross-legged on one end of my bed, kicking off my slippers. "Are you ready for something truly strange?"

"OK," she said, looking wary. "Try me. What's so weird about Mrs Okuda's neck?"

And so I told her. About the Red Cross woman, disappeared or invisible at our door. The icy breeze that had swept into our house. My brother's strange coughing. The meaning of the marks we'd seen on Mrs Okuda's neck. But I didn't stop there. I told her about the way a nukekubi could leave its body to fly screaming through the night, searching for human flesh. And I told her of my darkest fear: that something had found us, travelled all the way from Japan, to wreak evil upon me and my family. Cait listened the whole time without interrupting, which was something of a miracle for her. Then it finally got too much.

"Whoah." She held up her hands in two stop signs. "I get all the other stuff, about the flying head people and Mrs Okuda, however creepy that might be. But I don't get why she'd come all

the way from Japan just to haunt you. Why wouldn't she haunt some other family, back in Japan? She didn't need to travel this far."

Cait had a point. And I didn't have an answer. Why would she leave Japan and come to England? What was so special about us, the Takeshitas? We were just another ordinary family, as far as I was concerned.

"I don't know." I looked across at my friend. She had a thoughtful look on her freckled face.

"Well," she said at last. "I guess that's not important. What we have to do is figure out how to stop her. We can figure out why she's here later on."

"Then you'll help?" I asked, hardly daring to hope.

"Sure." Cait grinned. "It's gotta be better than doing homework."

"All right!" We were a team! Partners against crime! I reached across to high-five her, and she nearly tipped over the chair.

"So now what do we do?"

"Now we…"

But I didn't know. The nukekubi could be anywhere. She could be watching our house right this minute. She could be planning something for tomorrow at school, or worse, for this very night.

We had to keep our doors and windows shut tight.

"Maybe we should wait for my dad to get back," I said, feeling very small. "He might suggest something."

"He knows about these cut-throat demon things?"

"Well, yes." Anyone Japanese knew about nukekubi. But only some, like my Baba, actually believed. What about my dad? Which was he?

We were both silent for a bit, thinking. Cait got up and walked across to my window, pulling aside the cream curtains. "It's still snowing," she said. "Look at it! I'm glad we're not walking home in that."

"Careful, Cait," I said. "She could be out there, watching." I slipped back into my slippers and padded across to the window. Cait was right. Outside it was getting dark and the street lamps were turning the falling snow into a yellow glow. The street was empty: no people, no moving cars. Just car-shaped blobs of snow parked on both sides of the road.

"Maybe we should wait till tomorrow," Cait said. "Take another look at Okuda, in the light. It's kind of dark to be thinking that flesh-eating monsters could be out there right now." She tried to laugh, but I could tell she was scared.

I was scared too. I moved away from the window, back to the bed. I was thinking of my mum, alone in the hospital, and of Kazu, his little cough still audible from below.

"What the…?" Cait exclaimed. She sounded excited. "Come and look at this, Miku. It's like a giant face, in the sky. It's like one of those cloud shapes on a sunny day, only this is a snow shape. It looks just like someone's massive head."

I scrambled back to the window, dreading what might be there. But it wasn't Okuda's head. Instead, hanging in the sky like a giant moon, was the murky shape of someone else's head. I could see its heavy eyebrows, the dark shadow of its eyes, the coil and wave of its hair. I couldn't tell if it was a man or a woman, but it definitely wasn't Mrs Okuda. It just hung there, with the wind blowing its ghostly black hair into the snow. It seemed to be right outside our window.

I held Cait's arm tight and we watched it in silence. It didn't move, it didn't try to speak. It just floated in the dusk, as big as a hundred heads all bunched together.

"Maybe it's just the snow clouds?" Cait whispered. But we both knew it wasn't.

We watched it for maybe a minute, then there was

the scream of an ambulance in the main street, and the hanging face vanished. It just faded away, folding back into the dark and the falling snow.

"What. Was. That?" Cait asked, speaking each word very slowly.

"I dunno. But I don't think we can wait till morning to find out. We have to ask my dad, and tonight."

A sharp rap at the door startled both of us.

"Girls. Can I come in?"

CHAPTER SIX

I looked across at Cait, and she nodded. It certainly sounded like Mrs Williams at the door, and all the doors and windows had been locked. You'd have to think we were safe in our own house.

"Sure," I called out. "Come in."

The door opened and Mrs Williams walked in. She looked around, searching for somewhere to sit. Cait and I moved quickly from the window to sit on the bed, leaving Mrs Williams the chair.

"Thank you, dears," she said. "I just thought I should come up. We need to have a talk."

I looked down at the stitching on my bedspread. I loved having a bed, a real bed, that you could sit on and be tucked into. In Japan we'd only ever had futons, rolling them out each night to sleep on the tatami floor. Sometimes I missed the smell of straw and the cosy feel of sleeping in a sandwich of thick futon mattress and puffy futon quilt. But I never missed having to fold it all away the next morning.

"I've just had a call from your father," Mrs Williams said. "He's stuck at work. His train isn't running and the buses are all cancelled because of the snow. He and some colleagues are going to stay at a hotel tonight, the roads just aren't safe…"

I sneaked a look at Cait. Already the bottom was falling out of our plan. Dad would be no help tonight.

"I told your mother I'd watch Kazu till your dad came home," Mrs Williams said, "but it's just that Andrew will be home tonight and I'd really like to keep an eye on him too. I know you must think he's all grown up, but to me he's still just a little boy. I don't like to leave him alone on a night like this…"

"That's OK, Mrs Williams." I knew what she was getting at. "I can look after Kazu by myself. I've done it heaps of times." This last bit wasn't exactly true, but I had looked after him once while Mum had nipped out to the shops. Although that was before my supply teacher had turned out to be a nukekubi demon.

"Oh no, dear," Mrs Williams said, shocked. "I don't think that would be right at all. I couldn't leave you and little Kazu alone, especially when he's ill. That would never do. Perhaps you should come over to our place for the night…"

"Don't worry, Mrs Williams," Cait piped up. "I'll be here too. I don't expect my dad will be able to pick me up either, so I'll have to stay here or at yours, and I think all of us sleeping at yours might be a bit of a crowd, don't you?"

Mrs Williams looked uncertain. "Well…"

"We'd only be next door," Cait added. "You could call us any time to check we were OK."

"I suppose," said Mrs Williams.

"OK then," said Cait, getting up from the bed. "I guess we can heat some leftovers for dinner, hey Miku?"

"Sure," I mumbled. "I'll put some rice in the cooker. There's some veggies left from last night. Mum's got all the dressings and stuff. Plus there's always toast if we get hungry later on."

"Well…" said Mrs Williams again.

Cait knew we were winning. "OK then," she said. "We better head downstairs if we're to take care of little Kazu and get dinner started. You've got our number then, Mrs Williams?"

Mrs Williams nodded, and followed Cait and me downstairs. Kazu was still on the sofa, coughing and watching TV. He hardly looked up when

Mrs Williams gathered her things and leaned over to give him a hug goodbye.

"Well, if you're sure you're OK…"

"We're sure. Thanks for your help so far. We'll call if we need anything."

We bustled Mrs Williams towards the door. This time I was careful to pull a chair across so I could climb up and peek through the peephole.

"What are you doing, dear?" Mrs Williams asked. "Are you sure you'll be all right?"

"Better safe than sorry," Cait chimed.

The corridor was clear.

"Thanks, Mrs Williams," we chorused. "Say hi to Andrew."

She was out in a jiffy, and we were careful to shut and lock the door behind her.

It was suddenly quiet. We were alone: me, Cait, and my little brother, still coughing on the sofa.

"Wow," I said. "I guess that's that."

"Yep." Cait looked determined. "Now we're free to work on this Okuda problem. Let's heat a pizza and get started on a plan."

We headed to the kitchen. I felt so lucky, I couldn't believe it. Cait was seriously into all this. She was going to help. "You really believe me, all this stuff?"

"Sure," she said. "Why not? We have our own demons here, vampires and werewolves and leprechauns and kelpies. There's no reason why your demons wouldn't be just as real as ours."

I was confused. Vampires and werewolves I'd heard of, but leprechauns and kelpies?

Cait saw my look. "Not now," she grinned. "Let's deal with one set of demons at a time."

I grinned back, then opened the freezer. "Hawaiian or pepperoni?"

Just then there was another knock at the door.

Cait and I shared a cautious glance. There'd been no one out there just seconds ago. I was getting a bit sick of all these surprises.

"Probably Mrs Williams," I mouthed.

She nodded, and together we headed to the front door. I climbed back on the chair to look through the peephole. There was someone out there all right. But it wasn't Mrs Williams.

Through the warped glass I could see a man, dressed in a suit. His brown hair was thin on top and he kept checking his watch, as if he was in a rush.

Could it be? He was very early.

"I think it's your dad," I whispered, getting down so Cait could climb up to confirm.

She took a quick peek. "Hey, Dad," she yelled

through the door, getting down from the chair nearly as quickly as she'd climbed up. When she opened the door, sure enough, Mr O'Neill was standing there, dusting the snow off his clothes and stamping his feet against the cold.

"Cait," he said, pulling his daughter into a hug. "Hello, Miku."

I nodded, not wanting a hug. My family weren't as big on hugging as the O'Neills.

"Isn't the weather dreadful?" he said. "I didn't think I'd make it. The roads are a mess. Have you got your things? We shouldn't stick around too long. The snow's still coming down out there."

"OK," said Cait, looking at me uncertainly. "It's just that…"

Then the phone rang. Perfect timing.

"I'll get it," I said, leaving Cait and her dad alone to figure out whether she'd be able to stay the night. I was really hoping he'd say yes. I didn't like the idea of me and Kazu alone all night with who knew what kind of demons lurking around outside. The way this day had been going, there could be almost anything out there. And Cait was always a good person to have on your side.

Together we'd figure out a way to defeat the nukekubi, cure my brother of his sudden illness and protect the house from any other supernatural guests.

I reached the phone on the fifth ring. Kazu hadn't moved, he was still glued to the box. One day he'd be old enough to be useful, but not yet, and not with that awful cough.

"Hello?" I said, picking up the phone. Mum had taught me never to answer the phone with my name, just in case it was a lunatic kidnapper on the other end. If only she'd been more careful about lunatic demons. But this time it wasn't a kidnapper. I even recognised the voice.

"Miku," the voice said. "How's it going?"

My heart stopped. I felt as if I was trapped in some sort of scary movie, the kind Mum would never let me watch on a Friday night.

"Hello?" I whispered. "Mr O'Neill?"

CHAPTER SEVEN

"Miku." The voice sounded relieved. "I don't suppose Cait's with you, is she? I've only just heard that school was let out early, so I'm hoping she went home with you. It's just that the buses and trains are all down and I can't find a way to pick her up tonight. I think it might be safer if she stays the night with you. Would that be OK?"

I tried to speak but couldn't make my tongue and mouth work together properly.

"Miku? Is everything OK?" Mr O'Neill's voice sounded worried. "Cait is with you, isn't she? Is she OK?"

Dazed, I began walking down the hall towards the front door. On the phone, Mr O'Neill was getting anxious. I had to make my voice work.

"Yes," I stammered. "Yes, everything's OK. She's right here."

And she was. When I reached the front door, Cait was standing there, with Mr O'Neill and her schoolbag. She didn't look happy.

"Dad says we have to go," she said. "Sorry."

The Mr O'Neill standing at our door nodded. "It'll be best if we get going now, Miku. Thanks for looking after Cait."

The Mr O'Neill on the phone spoke again. "Are you sure everything's OK? Can I speak to Cait please?"

"Who's on the phone?" Cait asked, catching the look on my face. "What's wrong, Miku? Is it your mum?"

I couldn't speak. I just stared at the Mr O'Neill at our door. Then I stared at the phone, now bleating with Mr O'Neill's concern.

"Miku? Miku? Can I speak to Cait please?"

Whatever was happening, it couldn't be good. I had to think fast. "Can we have a minute, Mr O'Neill?" I asked, talking to the man standing in the door.

"Sure," he said. "But make it quick, please, girls. I'll wait for you in the hallway."

He stepped outside and Cait pounced on me.

"What is it?" she asked. "Who's on the phone?"

I took a deep breath, then I told her.

"It's your dad."

"What?" I could tell she didn't believe me.

There was only one way to convince her. "Here," I said, passing her the phone. "It's your dad."

"But," Cait stammered, looking from the phone to the man waiting in the hallway. She put the phone to her ear.

"Hello?"

"Oh, thank God," Mr O'Neill's voice sounded loud with relief. "What's going on, Cait? Are you in trouble?"

Cait paled for a moment. Her freckles drained of all colour and her eyes grew wide. Then she took a deep breath.

"No," she said, her voice airy and light. "Everything's fine. Sorry, it's just that we're distracted. Miku's little brother is sick. You remember Keiji?"

"Keiji," I heard Mr O'Neill stop. "Keiji?" Cait and I both held our breath. "I thought it was Kazu," he said.

"That's what I said," Cait covered. "Kazu. So yeah, he's ill and Miku's a bit worried. Would it be OK if I stayed here tonight?"

I waited for Mr O'Neill's answer, keeping an eye on the Mr O'Neill in the hallway. He was facing the outer door, kicking at a bit of loose carpet. He had Cait's bag and looked ready to leave at any moment. My stomach churned. Something was very wrong.

"OK, thanks, Dad," Cait was finishing up. "Thanks, take care. I love you too."

She hung up the phone, raised an eyebrow at me, then turned to look at the Mr O'Neill in our hallway.

"Dad," she said.

"Yes, love?"

"I'm ready to go now..."

"Great," said Mr O'Neill. "We're parked just outside."

"...But," Cait continued, "do you mind if I say a quick goodbye to Miku's little brother before we go? You remember Keiji?"

"Oh yes, Keiji," the Mr O'Neill replied. "I hear he's not well, poor little boy. Say a quick goodbye, and then we really have to hit the road."

Cait and I exchanged glances, then ran off down the hall towards the living room.

"Keiji," Cait hissed. "He said Keiji, not Kazu. And how did he know Kazu was sick? And how'd he get into the building anyway? He doesn't have a key. I don't think he's the real thing, Miku."

"Then what is he?" I asked. "And what's he doing in our hallway?"

The TV was still on when we reached the living room, but Kazu was nowhere to be seen.

"Kazu," I called, hunting in the kitchen and under the table. "Kazu? Perhaps he went upstairs?"

We raced upstairs, running through rooms and searching under beds. "Kazu?" I cried. "Kazu?"

I checked in Mum and Dad's room, where we were never allowed to go. "Kazu-chan?"

But we couldn't find him.

"Come on," Cait said. "Downstairs, that guy, my dad. He's still down there."

We took the stairs two at a time, nearly falling in the rush to get down. When we reached the front door, Mr O'Neill was still waiting in the hallway. He had his back turned to us, still kicking at the loose bit of carpet.

"Who are you?" Cait cried. "Where's Kazu?"

For a moment the Mr O'Neill didn't turn around, didn't look up.

"Where's my little brother?" I hissed. "What have you done with him?"

"Dad?" Cait asked, hesitating. "What have you done with Kazu?"

The Mr O'Neill made a strange sighing noise, then kicked again at the rough carpet seam before turning to look at us.

Cait screamed. I screamed. We both screamed so loud I was sure Mrs Williams would come running. Then we doubled back into the house, slamming and locking the door behind us. I pushed the chair up against the door for added protection, then climbed up on it to look through the peephole. Cait was too scared even to peek.

"What was that?" she panted. "What was that thing?"

I looked through the hole. "It's still out there," I said. "No, hang on, it's leaving."

Whatever it was, it wasn't Mr O'Neill.

When the thing had turned around, its face had been a perfect blank, smooth as an eggshell, with no eyes, no nose, no mouth. No nothing, just a blank sheet of skin, covering everything that had been there before. All trace of Mr O'Neill had been smoothed away from that face.

I watched the thing as it escaped into the snow, closing the outside door behind it.

"It's gone," I said.

Cait was shaking. "What was it?"

At first I had no idea, then something my Baba had told me came tumbling back from my darkest memories. "A noppera-bō," I said, feeling angry at myself for getting so scared. "I should've known."

"A noppera-what? Why did it look like my dad?"

"A noppera-bō. Baba told me about them once. They're mostly harmless."

Cait snorted. "Harmless? I nearly had a heart attack. What was it doing?"

"I did say mostly." I almost grinned. "They really don't do much except scare people. I don't know what one was doing here... Unless..."

Why would a noppera-bō come to our house? What business did such a demon have here?

And then I remembered my brother. "Kazu? Where is he?"

I jumped off the chair and tried to run down the hall, but Cait stopped me, grabbing my arm. "Hang on. He has to be in here somewhere. He can't have just disappeared. Let's do a proper search."

Cait was right. We shouldn't panic. We had to do a thorough search of the whole apartment. And we did.

But she was also wrong. She said Kazu couldn't have just disappeared. But as far as we could tell, he wasn't anywhere. He had gone. There was no sign of him, just a place on the sofa still warm from where he'd been watching TV.

I sat down, touching the warm spot and fighting back tears. "Where can he be? I just know she's taken him."

"She who?" Cait asked. "No one could've got in here."

"Mrs Okuda," I said, hopeless tears sitting heavy in my eyes. "The nukekubi. She can go anywhere. I just know she's got him."

Cait sat down next to me, stroking my hair. "Then we'll get him back, that's all," she said. "We'll get him back tonight. We'll stop all this. Your brother missing, some freaky spirit pretending to be my dad, this bizarre snowstorm, Mr Lloyd with chicken pox. There's too much weird stuff happening and it's got to stop. We'll get Kazu back tonight, Miku, I promise."

CHAPTER EIGHT

"First things first," Cait said. "We eat a pizza. And you tell me everything you know about these nukekubi. None of these other demon things we've seen seem to eat people, so I think Mrs Okuda should be our biggest priority. She might even be their leader. Somehow, she must be the key."

I had to agree. Even the crazy snow situation seemed to have been triggered by Okuda's arrival. "OK." I walked to the kitchen. "But one thing: they're not people. They just look like people. They're exactly like that noppera-bō. Nukekubi are demons, but they take the shape of ordinary people."

"OK," said Cait, following me into the kitchen. "So they're demons. What next? How do we know if we're looking at a nukekubi or a real person?"

"Easy. The red marks on their necks when it's daytime. And airborne screaming heads if it's not."

We both laughed, but it really wasn't funny. I pulled a pepperoni pizza from the freezer and stuck it in the oven, turning the dial to 180 like I'd seen Mum do stacks of times before. It was a Sunday night favourite.

"Screaming?" Cait asked. We both watched the yellow oven light, waiting for the first smell of cheese to float through the oven door.

"Yep. They scream so they can scare you more, freak you out and make you do something stupid. Then they swoop down and tear chunks from your throat with their teeth."

"Right," said Cait. "Don't panic if I see a man-eating flying head. Good. This is going well. Is there anything useful?"

And then I remembered something Baba had told me, many years before. For the first time since Kazu got sick, I began to feel that maybe we had a chance.

"Their bodies," I said. "While their heads are out screaming and flying around, their bodies are asleep, just waiting for their heads to come back."

"That," said Cait, "is disgusting."

"Yeah, but think about it. If we can find her body while her head is away, we can destroy it, or move it or something, and then she'd be stuck. She'd be banished, or finished, or whatever happens to nukekubi when they die."

I opened the oven to check on the pizza.

"Still ages to go," said Cait. "So is that our plan?"

"What?" I closed the oven door.

"We pick a time when her head will be flying around..." Cait said.

"Tonight," I interrupted. "It's always at night, and Kazu can't wait till tomorrow."

"Tonight," Cait agreed. "And then we find where she's hidden her body. And then we destroy it, defeating her and all the other demons."

It sounded so simple when Cait said it. I was so glad her real dad had let her stay.

"Cool," I said, nodding. "That's our plan."

"So where do we start?"

"Where do you reckon her body is?"

"Where do *you* reckon?" Cait asked. "Where do they usually hang out?"

"Well," I said, thinking hard. "She can't have an ordinary home, cos she won't have any real money. But she'd have to be somewhere safe, where no one would find her. Somewhere where there's hardly any people wandering around at night."

"School," Cait said. "We saw her there first. It's easy for her to be there during the day, and it's empty at night. She could leave her body under a desk or in a broom cupboard or something."

"School," I agreed. Cait was brilliant. "That's got to be it. But we have to get there now. Kazu's already in trouble."

"We'll go tonight," Cait said. "But first, let's eat pizza. We can't fight demons when we're starving."

While the pizza cooked we ran round the house, finding hats and jackets to protect us from the snow. I put a handful of cedar leaves in each of our pockets, just in case. Unlike my mum, Cait didn't scoff or laugh. Then we swallowed the pizza so fast I hardly chewed, and I burnt the roof of my mouth on the cheese.

"Right," Cait said, wiping tomato sauce from her chin. "Is there anything else we need?"

She looked set for an Antarctic expedition, all trussed up in Mum's old jacket with one of Dad's beanies. I knew I must look the same, although my jacket probably looked a little better.

"Nope," I said. "We're ready."

"OK."

We were standing just inside our front door, next to the pile of shoes we'd left earlier.

"I guess this is it." I slipped out of my slippers and put on my shoes.

Cait did the same, arranging her green cat slippers neatly on the rack, just how Mum always left them. "I guess so."

I climbed up one last time on the chair, peering out of our door into the hallway. "It's all clear."

The hallway was still empty when we locked the front door behind us.

We made it to the outside door without meeting anyone, but almost at once our troubles began. The door wouldn't open. I tried again and again, but it hardly budged. Were we trapped in our own building?

"The snow?" Cait suggested. This time she helped me push on the door, and it swung a bit further open.

She was right. Outside it was still snowing and the snow was piling up, almost blocking our front door.

"Again," I said. "One, two, three."

We both heaved and the door edged open enough for us to get through. Outside the snowy day had turned to dark, dark night, and the snow was still coming down. The streets were completely empty. Even the street lamps seemed to have lost their colour. The entire world was cloaked in white snow, turned eerie gray by the darkness. I shivered.

"Come on," Cait said. "Let's make this quick."

CHAPTER NINE

Ten minutes later we were creeping through the school grounds, two lines of footprints trailing behind us in the snow. The cold was biting at my nose and draining my hands, but the rest of me was warm with excitement and action. We didn't bother trying to open the front door to the school. It would almost certainly be locked.

"She won't be using doors," I guessed. "It's too obvious. She'd be scared someone will see her. Plus nukekubi don't need doors."

"So how does she get in and out?" Cait asked. "What should we be looking for?"

"Dunno. But we'll know it when we see it."

And then we did. Through the falling snow we spotted a window, a few rooms down from our classroom. It was propped open when it should have been firmly closed.

"A window," we both said, heading for the telltale opening.

"But no one's been in or out of here since the snow started," Cait hissed, pointing at the unmarked snow beneath the window. She was right. There were no marks or imprints in the snow, but I hadn't been expecting any.

"Flying heads don't leave footprints," I said, trying to sound brave. "The rest of her body will be in here somewhere." I peered through the gap to check the room beyond. No sign of a headless nukekubi. It was deserted, filled with empty desks and chairs and paintings hanging on a clothes-line.

Together, Cait and I forced the window open a bit further. My frozen fingers were starting to hurt in the cold.

"You go first." Cait scanned the empty playground. "I'll keep an eye out for the flying head."

"It won't be back for hours yet," I said. "Not till morning." But I scrambled through the window all the same. It was freezing out there.

Inside the dark classroom it was just as cold, and deathly silent. The falling snow seemed to suck out any noise.

"You in?" Cait hissed from outside the window.

"Yep, coast is clear." I looked around, rubbing my hands together to get the blood back into them. A few seconds later, Cait tumbled in through the window. "Anything out there?" I asked.

"Nope, no one followed us." Cait stood up and dusted the snow from her jacket. "Let's get moving though." She slid the window back and clicked the lock. "Even if her head does fly back early, it won't be getting in through this window."

I grinned. We were actually doing it. We were hunting the nukekubi.

"Where to?" Cait whispered.

"Our classroom?" I wasn't sure, but it was the place we'd last seen her, and as good a place as any to start looking.

Cait nodded, and together we headed across the empty classroom to the hallway door. I could hear my heart beating so loudly I was sure Cait could hear it too. I peered around the door, searching the darkness for what lay beyond.

Nothing moved. The whole corridor was silent, empty.

"Come on," I whispered.

We sneaked out, scurrying with shoes squeaking to our classroom. It was freezing in the corridor and our breath made little clouds as we moved.

I half expected them to turn to ice and fall cracking to the floor as we walked. We went straight to our classroom without stopping, just like when the corridors were full of kids and teachers and schoolbags. Except now the whole place was empty, as silent and frozen as the moon.

The doorknob of our classroom door was frosted with tiny ice crystals. Cait turned it slowly, with such care that it didn't even squeak. She edged the door open, peeking one eye around to see inside the room.

I waited in the freezing corridor while Cait checked the room. After what seemed like forever, Cait swung the door completely open.

"I don't think she's here," she said, puffing a cloud of white with her breath.

We tiptoed into our classroom. It was like a graveyard – rows of empty desks, some with lonely pencils or forgotten books left on top, like sad offerings at a shrine. Mr Lloyd's desk was just like all the others: empty of life. And there was no sign of the nukekubi.

"Where would she be?" Cait asked, shivering.

I was shivering too. My frozen fingers were aching, and the cold seemed to be spreading. What were we doing here? Maybe I had imagined the red markings on Mrs Okuda's neck. Or maybe they were just mosquito bites, or a tattoo. She might be just an ordinary person who happened to like unusual bright red neck tattoos. I opened my mouth to ask Cait what she thought, but no sound came out. Instead, an awful wailing echoed from the corridor.

Cait jumped to attention, as if she'd been shot in some scene from an old Western movie. Then we both ran for the door, peering outside. I felt sick. This was it. There had to be something out there. The nukekubi was hunting.

But the corridor was empty and quiet once again.

"Was that her?" Cait hissed.

"Dunno. Maybe." I'd never heard one before. What did a nukekubi's hunting call sound like? Had we really thought this through before we came here all alone in the middle of the night to hunt a flying demon head?

The wail echoed again, this time a piercing scream that seemed to move up and down the corridor like a wave.

I grabbed Cait's arm and hung on. "It's a ghost. There's nothing out there to make that noise. It's got to be a ghost."

I'd heard Baba talk of ghosts. Yurei, 'faint spirits' in English, usually someone who'd died horribly, who couldn't make it to the afterlife.

A shot of cold passed through me. There had to be a ghost walking with us. An angry ghost by the sound of it. I wanted to run but the cold had frozen me to the spot. My nose began to tingle and burn and I could feel my blood cooling, sending icy messages to my heart.

The screaming came once again, but it changed mid-way, becoming a cracking sound instead, metallic and ringing like a bell. Suddenly it didn't sound like any ghost I'd ever heard of. But it still didn't sound friendly. And if it wasn't a ghost, what was it?

More loud gonging sounds echoed along the corridor, seeming to come from the walls themselves. It was as if we were trapped inside a massive temple bell on New Year's Eve. The sounds kept getting louder until something seemed to break. A crash like thunderclaps exploded all around us, up and down the corridor and, horror of horrors, even from the classroom behind us.

I swung round to see what was coming up behind us, but could see nothing that could have caused the noise.

"That's no ghost," Cait guessed. "I think it's gunshots. Someone's in here with a gun."

Just then the noises stopped. And, just as suddenly, the cold lifted. My blood started flowing again.

"The pipes," I guessed. "There's no ghost, and no gun. It's the pipes. They've frozen. They've burst with the cold."

"What?"

It felt like a better idea than gunshots and ghosts, but I still wasn't sure. "The cold," I said. "It can freeze water in the pipes. Like when you freeze a Coke can in the fridge. The water expands and the pipe explodes. There's water pipes all through the school."

"Exploding pipes?" Cait didn't sound convinced. She unzipped her jacket as her face flushed in the growing warmth.

"Sure, why not?" I unzipped my own jacket and ripped off my beanie. "That screeching, the gunshots, I bet that was the water expanding through the pipes until they exploded with the pressure."

Cait took off her own beanie. "If it's frozen pipes, then they're not going to be frozen for long. Something's messing with the temperature in here."

We looked around, remembering suddenly why we were here.

"Can she do that?" Cait asked. "The nukekubi?"

I shook my head. "No, I don't think so. It's got to be something else." I knew there was something my Baba had told me, something else. But it floated just out of reach, a kite on the wind.

"So how will we know if it's burst pipes that made all that noise?" Cait interrupted my thoughts.

But before I could answer, a dripping sound came from the classroom behind us. Almost at once more drips echoed from the corridor. Gone were the ringing and screaming of tortured pipes. Instead we could have been in a bathhouse. The sound of dripping water was everywhere. Five minutes ago we were freezing solid, now it was warm enough to go without a jacket.

"The water's melting," Cait said. She pulled off her scarf. "This is ridiculous."

The drips grew into trickles, like a hundred taps not turned off properly.

"The whole water system's busted," I said.

"What happens now?" Cait asked, watching as the trickles formed torrents and water began to gush from broken pipes up and down the corridor.

"I dunno."

"Will she like all this water?" Cait asked.

I stepped backwards as the water advanced towards our open door. "No, I don't think so. Baba never said."

I stepped back again, this time splashing right into a puddle. Behind us the floor of the classroom was shiny with water. More water was pouring in from the broken pipes, forming a fountain that was gushing and trickling its way into a flood.

Cait climbed on to the nearest desk. "I think we're going to get a little wet," she said, her legs dangling as water rushed around and under the table legs below.

Shoes wet, I jumped up on the desk next to Cait. We watched as the water from our classroom floor inched closer to the door. "We're going to be in so much trouble."

"Deep trouble," Cait laughed at her own joke.

"But really it's not so deep," I said, looking down. "Perhaps we should make a run for it?"

"What about the flying head?"

But I didn't have time to reply. Another thunderclap echoed as water from the corridor rushed to meet the water from our classroom. Great. The temperature had stopped rising, but now the whole school was flooding. And we still had to find my brother, defeat a flesh-eating demon, and get home before Mrs Thompson or the plumber caught us sneaking around the school after dark.

The classroom window had fogged up, but I could see giant snowflakes bashing against the glass. Inside it was as warm as a summer's day. "This is so weird." I racked my brains, trying again to think of what it was my Baba had told me. Something about the weather... Something important.

"Totally," Cait said, looking around. Each desk had formed a little island in the growing ocean. "We're surrounded. It's like something's set out to trap us."

Chapter Ten

Five minutes later, when the water had stopped rising, we had a new problem on our hands.

"What on earth is that?" Cait asked, staring in dread as water began arriving in waves at our classroom door, causing mini-tsunamis to rush against the walls of our classroom. The water was behaving like surf at the ocean, forming waves that raced through the door, each curling after the next.

"Flood's getting worse?" I asked, my teeth chattering despite the warm temperature.

"No," Cait said. "I think something's coming."

The waves were growing larger. We could see the bulk of them as they pummelled past our open door, with just the smaller waves pushing sideways into our classroom. I didn't know what to do. We were perched like helpless sailors on our school-desk desert islands.

"Perhaps we should run for it," I said again. "It could be her. Who cares about wet shoes?"

But it was too late. The waves had slowed and now just a few cautious ripples were rolling into the classroom. The thing, whatever it was, was nearly here.

"Hello?" said a voice from down the hall. It was a woman's voice, and not Mrs Okuda. I heaved a sigh of relief, but I didn't answer. Cait stayed silent too.

The ripples started again, pushing towards us. A woman's face appeared round the classroom door. "Hello?" she asked again. The face was quite young and beautiful, with a small nose and wide almond eyes, but both Cait and I screamed anyway. Cait stood up on her desk, trying to edge backwards and away.

"Children?" The woman seemed surprised to see us. "But what are you doing here?"

I was asking myself exactly the same question. We could have been at home eating pizza. But I couldn't take my eyes off her, for although the woman's features were as pretty as any of the girls in the magazines, her skin was bright green and shiny like a frog's. She had long black hair that hung wet around her head and her tongue was red and forked.

It seemed to quiver like a snake's, as if she was using it to smell us out.

She came closer, gliding like a serpent. As she approached, more ripples lapped against the legs of our school desks.

Cait made a tiny choking noise. Her eyes were bulging and she seemed unable to speak.

I wasn't surprised. Being eaten by a massive snake-woman-demon-thing had not been part of our plan. I just stood there, silent, and waited for whatever came next.

The woman was wet all over and dressed in red, with green scaly arms reaching out of each sleeve. Her skin, green with streaks of mustard yellow, was clearly visible beneath the transparent fabric.

"Oh, I'm so sorry." She slid back a little. She didn't seem to have legs, just a long, snake-like body that disappeared into the corridor. "I didn't mean to disturb you. I didn't realise there'd be more children here."

For that was the worst of it. Worse than her green skin and forked tongue, worse than the way her body seemed to melt into a legless lizard. In her scaly green arms, this dragon demon held Kazu, my darling brother, tiny and trusting and asleep.

"Oh, but it's you," the dragon woman said, suddenly smiling up at me with warm, blood-red eyes. "Miku." She slid further into the room, her snake's body seemingly endless as it extended through the door and into the corridor. At the point where her jacket ended, her skin turned to red and shone wet and naked in the moonlight, rippling as it entered the room.

I could only gurgle back. This dragon knew me. And it had Kazu. And now it would have us too.

"It is Miku, isn't it?" the woman asked, her smile revealing two pointed fangs. "Takeshita Miku. I've heard so much about you. I was a great fan of your grandmother's."

Slowly, like a statue come to life, I nodded. What was this thing? What did it know of Baba?

"She did so much for your family," the woman continued, hissing a little as her scarlet tongue flashed in and out. "Such a tragedy that she passed away. Still, she lived to a good age. It's your turn now."

My turn? I had no idea what this monster was talking about, but I had finally found my voice. "My brother," I said. "Give him back."

"Oh, of course," she said, looking down at the sleeping Kazu. "But not yet. Not yet. I need him still."

"Give him back," I demanded, a little louder this time. "Give him back now." Now I had my voice I was trying for my courage as well. My words sounded strange, echoing off the walls and the water.

"But do you not know me?" the dragon woman asked, surprised. "The zashiki-warashi has sent me."

Zashiko had sent her, all the way from our house back in Japan? The mischievous child ghost, who had moved my pillow and swung my bedroom light in the night? I didn't believe it. Zashiko had always protected our family from evil, but this misshapen demon monster had stolen Kazu.

"He's my brother," I said. "We've come to take him home." I had hoped to sound heroic and strong, but in the face of this demon, I sounded almost apologetic.

"But you cannot take him from me now." The dragon woman looked concerned. "I have travelled so far. I have achieved so much. I have discovered the nukekubi, fought the yuki-onna. We are so close to victory, you and I."

Victory? You and I?

Cait shot me a look that said, plain as day, *you know this woman-thing?*

No. I shook my head. I'd never seen her before in my life. The yuki-onna, the thing she claimed to have fought, I'd heard of that. Another demon my Baba had talked about. But there wasn't time to think of that now. We needed Kazu back, and we needed to go home. We'd been crazy to try this alone.

"Give him to me," I said. "In the name of my Baba. In the name of Zashiko, our zashiki-warashi." If this dragon claimed to know Baba and Zashiko, perhaps that could work in our favour.

The dragon woman made a strange sound, a kind of watery whimper. "But the plan. The nukekubi. She is here, somewhere in the school. I must take your brother to her."

Take Kazu to the Okuda-monster? This was the last straw. There was no way Zashiko had sent this disgusting creature. It was a lie, another trick, like the Mr O'Neill noppera-bō. I might not be the world's best sister, but I drew the line at feeding my brother to a flying demon head. I decided right then and there: there was no way I was going to let anyone take Kazu anywhere near the nukekubi, and especially not this scaly green snake-demon thing. Even if my life depended on it.

"Give him to me," I commanded. This time my

voice came out booming and hot, like Mr Lloyd's when he was mad at Alex.

The dragon woman squirmed. Kazu wriggled in her arms, still sleeping soundly. "It's not right," she said. "Zashiko has a plan..." But she slithered closer, her green arms extended slightly, holding Kazu out over the water.

I moved to the edge of the desk, close enough to reach out and touch Kazu. "Give him to me."

The dragon woman moved closer still, dangling Kazu like bait over a shark pit. "Are you sure, Takeshita Miku? Are you ready? Can you take him?"

I didn't answer right away. Instead I grabbed Kazu as quickly as I could, cringing away from the cool touch of the woman's scaly skin. "Yes, very sure. I'm ready."

Kazu felt warm and alive, soft and heavy in my arms. We'd done it! He didn't wake. I started to dream that we might make it home, me and Kazu and Cait.

The dragon woman hadn't moved. She stood there, watching Kazu as I held him. Her red eyes had narrowed, like a snake watching a mouse. It felt weird that she hadn't backed away, but at least she hadn't come any closer.

Cait had had enough. "Thanks for that," she said.

"We're leaving now." But though she sounded as if she meant it, she didn't move an inch. Neither did the dragon woman.

"Leave us," Cait tried again. "We're going home."

But the woman didn't even twitch.

And I wasn't going anywhere. Kazu was breathing peacefully in my arms, but he seemed to be getting heavier every second. He seemed to be turning into lead, becoming heavier and heavier, until my arms were aching with the weight of him. I didn't care. I took a deep breath and hung on.

"Hey, Kazu," I crooned. "It's OK now, I've got you. We're going to take you home."

"Come on, Miku," said Cait, still eyeing the dragon woman warily. "Let's get out of here."

But I couldn't take a step. Kazu was growing heavier still. My arms felt as if they were being stretched, pulled down to the ground by their tremendous load.

Kazu looked just as peaceful as ever, but my arm muscles were burning up and my legs had started trembling with the weight. "It's OK, Kazu," I said, gritting my teeth. "It's OK."

But it wasn't. I was shaking with the strain now. How much longer could I hold him?

I looked up at the dragon woman. "What have you done to him? Let him go."

"You care for this child?" she asked, eyes glittering and tongue waving in the air.

"Yes," I gasped. I was staggering. "I love him, he's my brother." I didn't think I could carry Kazu's weight much longer.

"But you leave him sick and alone, coughing on the sofa…" the woman said.

"That was a mistake," I panted, my arms and legs ready to explode. "The amazake-baba, then the noppera-bō…" I cursed the spirits who had made Kazu ill, who had distracted us as we cared for him. And I cursed this dragon demon, who seemed to be crushing me under the weight of my own brother's body.

"No," the dragon woman reared up on her massive snake's body. She towered over me with her fangs shining in the moonlight. "It was you who left him. You who left him alone. Nobody did that but you."

My whole body was trembling as if under the weight of a thousand houses, but I refused to let Kazu go.

"OK," I panted. Kazu's weight was crushing my lungs, breaking my ribs. "OK. I shouldn't have left him. I was wrong. But that doesn't change anything. I still love him, and we're taking him back home with us, today."

With a mammoth effort, pulling strength and energy from places I didn't even know I had, I heaved Kazu's tiny body up a little higher, holding him close to my body and hanging on as if my whole life depended on it.

Suddenly, the weight was gone. Kazu seemed to float in my arms. He was back to normal, my ordinary sleeping brother.

The dragon woman had returned to eye level. "Good," she said. "I see you care for this child properly, as all children deserve."

"What is going on?" Cait said. She seemed to have missed everything. "Come on, Miku, let's get out of here."

But now that I could move again, I wasn't so keen to leave. "Who are you?" I stared at the demon in front of me. Her scaly, shiny skin, her red eyes, the fangs and serpent's body.

The woman suddenly looked sad. "I am the nure-onna," she said. "The woman of the wet."

Yuki-onna I'd heard of, even my Mum knew stories of her. But the nure-onna? This was a first. Not even my Baba had mentioned her. "What are you doing here?" I demanded. "Why did you take my brother?"

"Hush," the woman said. "The nukekubi is still about, and it's nearly morning. Her head may return any moment."

"But why did you take him?" After all we'd been through, I wanted answers.

"He was sick and alone," she answered. "And I needed him. It was Zashiko's plan. I could care for him. You will see his cough is gone."

I looked down at Kazu. She was right. He did seem to be breathing easily, with no sign of his earlier illness.

"Quick," the woman hissed, red tongue darting. "The water drains, morning grows closer. Take him home and keep him safe. Do not come back to school today. I will deal with the nukekubi. She is causing only trouble."

The dragon woman was right. Outside the night was growing lighter, and inside the water had stopped gushing from the broken pipes. Slowly, the flood was withdrawing.

"I must go," the dragon woman said, sliding backwards out the door. "Go home at once. She will be back any moment, and she will be hunting for you."

CHAPTER ELEVEN

"What was that?" Cait blurted out as soon as the woman of the wet had gone. "This is getting way too weird, Miku."

I agreed. There were so many questions whirling in my own head. "The nure-onna," I whispered to myself, still holding Kazu safe in my arms. I'd never heard of her. And she said Zashiko had sent her?

"I have no idea," I answered Cait. "But I agree. It's getting too weird. We've got Kazu now. Let's do what she said and get out of here."

"I've been suggesting that for ages. What happened? You looked like you were going to collapse back there."

I shuddered at the memory of clinging to Kazu's massive, unnatural weight. "I'll explain on the way home. Let's move it."

The water hadn't quite receded, but who cared

about wet feet when a shiny-skinned dragon demon lurked in the corridors and a flesh-eating flying head could arrive back any minute?

"But she seemed to know you," Cait persisted. "And your Baba. And she seemed to know a whole lot about the nukekubi too."

We sloshed our way to a classroom window and I wiped a veil of fog from the glass. Outside everything was white, but at least it had stopped snowing. Something had stopped the snow, and that reminded me. The yuki-onna.

"Did you hear what she said?" I asked. "About that other demon?"

"Something," Cait said. "Yes. No. I can't remember all those Japanese names."

"She said she'd fought the yuki-onna," I said. "That's the woman of the snow. She's a famous demon, a big one, back in Japan."

"The yuki-onna? Great. What's she like then? Another giant serpent we have to fight?"

"No." I struggled to remember all the details. "She takes the shape of a beautiful lady, dressed all in white and with snow-white skin." Then it came to me. I remembered. "She's it," I exclaimed. "She's the one."

"The one what?"

"The one with the weather. She's the snow woman. She needs snow to survive, she can freeze things with her breath. I bet it was the yuki-onna who made the snowstorm, who cracked the pipes."

"Why would she do all that?"

I grimaced. Cait wasn't going to like my answer. "Well..."

"She's not another child-eater, is she?"

"Not exactly."

"Good. So she can't be that bad." Cait breathed a sigh of relief and turned her attention to the window. "This one?" She picked the nearest window, the one I'd wiped clean from the fog.

"Sure." Together we struggled to flick the latch and open the window. I kept quiet for a bit, cradling Kazu in one arm the whole time. There was no way I was leaving him anywhere ever again.

"So what does she do, then?" Cait asked, halfway through unlatching the window. "This snow lady. She freeze people to death?"

"Well..."

"What?" Cait stopped working and stared at me, incredulous. The window hung half-open. "She doesn't!"

I stroked Kazu's sleeping head. "Actually, she kind of does. She's some sort of lost soul.

Angry maybe. Some people say she sucks the life force from her victims."

"What?" Cait's face dropped. "This is mental. What are all these things? Why are they coming after you?"

I shook my head. "I dunno. But on the bright side, she's not around any more. Look." I pointed outside. "It's stopped snowing. Someone, or something, maybe even that nure-onna, has forced her back."

Cait struggled to release the last latch on the window. "Well, the snow lady can't be worse than the water lady. She was just plain scary. I vote these dragon people and snow demons fight their own battles from now on. Let's just get out of here." She flicked the last latch free with a solid click.

Cait swung the window wide. A gust of cold air raced into the humid classroom and we were staring out across a snowy white winterland. It was still night and everything was silent. Deathly still.

"Wow."

"Come on," Cait said, and she started to climb up into the window.

"Wait!" A flash of darkness, blacker than black, had caught my eye. It was outside. In the sky, in the treetops. I grabbed Cait's shoulder with my spare hand and she froze.

"She's out there, isn't she?"

"You saw it too?"

"Something flashed. In the sky."

"Could it be more snow?" I tried to think. "A bird?"

The black thing burst from the treetops and came whirling in a vacuum of light towards us.

"No!" Cait screamed and slammed the window shut, flicking the latches and backing away.

Something slammed teeth-first into the window. The glass shrieked like fingernails down a blackboard, but it didn't break. It was Mrs Okuda, or more correctly, Mrs Okuda's flying demon head.

I jumped backwards, following Cait in an attempt to get as far from the windows as possible.

"Now what?" Cait asked, her face white.

"I dunno." It was still dark, she'd come back too early. We were alone now, us against her. Unless… "We could find the nure-onna?" Maybe she was telling the truth about dealing with the yuki-onna, and the nukekubi. Maybe she could do the fighting for us?

Mrs Okuda's head smashed again into the glass, eyes rolling back in her head and teeth gnashing. Her shiny hair flew around her like a cape, and I could see the red marks at the bottom of her neck, the place where her head would reconnect to her body when she returned to wherever it was hidden.

"No way," Cait said. "All these demon people will have to sort themselves out. That water woman was half-dragon, Miku. Disgusting. And dangerous. Isn't there something else? Some other way to deal with this thing?"

The flying head shot again in our direction, a black comet through the white sky. This time it slammed so hard into the glass that the whole window shuddered. When it whirled away for another attack, it left a smear of red blood on the glass.

"Her body," I remembered. "She has a human body. We just need to find it, before her head does. If we can move or destroy the body, the nukekubi's power is gone."

"Right." Cait sprang into action. "Find the body. It's a plan. Let's get moving and get out of here."

I nodded, jumping down from the window on to the still-wet floor.

"We should split up," Cait said. "Save time. You take Kazu and go left, I'll go right. Let's check every classroom, every cupboard. The body's got to be in here somewhere."

"Split up?" I didn't like the idea of going alone, not with so many demons and spirits on the loose.

Okuda's head smashed again at the classroom window. In the moment of collision I could see everything, her skin pressed flat against the glass, the gnashing of her teeth, her dark eyes watching, always watching. And this time, the glass cracked.

"We don't have a choice," Cait said. "We need to find the body, and quickly."

A jagged crack spread through the glass, but the window didn't break. We were still safe, but for how much longer? The head whirled away, trailing long black hair behind it, then it turned in mid-air to attack again.

"OK then," I had to agree. "Let's go."

We raced to the classroom door. The corridors were empty but still shining and wet. "Good luck," I said. "We'll meet up again once the body's gone. Here, OK?"

"OK," Cait nodded. "One thing. You said 'move or destroy'. I won't be able to move a body on my own. So how do I destroy it?"

I hadn't thought that far ahead. "Fire? Drowning? I dunno. I think it's just like an ordinary body."

"You mean we have to kill it?" Cait looked horrified.

The sound of shattering glass prevented my answer. The classroom window was broken.

The nukekubi had smashed a fist-sized hole in the glass, not yet big enough for a head, but nearly.

"Go on! Good luck!"

Cait ran right. I ran left, cradling Kazu, still sleeping, in my arms. My footsteps splattered and boomed through the wet corridor and I could hear Cait's echoing as she ran the other way. I looked down at Kazu's trusting little face. Now we were truly alone. And I had no idea where to look for the body.

I ducked into the nearest classroom, jamming the door shut with a chair before starting the search. I checked under and behind desks, opened the wooden cupboard at the back of the class, the wooden cabinets along the side of the room. Nothing. No sign of Mrs Okuda's sleeping body. I could hear my heart pumping faster, drumming like the rhythm of a *taiko* drum.

"This is ridiculous," I said, talking more to myself than my sleeping brother. "There are dozens of classrooms just like this. We'll never find it this way. We need a plan."

I took a deep breath, tried to quiet the drumming in my chest. "We need a plan, Kazu."

But what was I expecting? Kazu wasn't going to answer. Even if he was awake and actually understood the danger, he wasn't going to say anything sensible. He was just a kid. A baby really. And he'd been so ill. He should be at home watching TV, giggling at the cartoons. Not being carried through a flooded school like a trussed-up radish. He just needed a place to sleep. Somewhere quiet and safe where he'd be protected from all this mess.

And that's when I had the idea.

"Come on, Kazu!"

I listened for a second at the door, then, with Kazu wrapped in one arm, I removed the chair I'd used to jam it shut and listened again. Silence. Then, slowly and ever so carefully, I turned the door handle and opened the door a crack and looked out. The corridor was still empty, still wet. I expected to see Okuda's purple-lipped head flying at me any second. But I had no time to imagine the worst. I had to get to Okuda's body, and fast.

Taking a careful hold of Kazu's little body, I slipped out of the classroom and headed down the corridor, towards the staff room, the school reception, the sick bay. I don't know why we hadn't thought of it earlier. The sick bay. With its calm, soft darkness, and the full-length bed. It even had pillows and sheets and a blanket. It had to be. Where else would a demon supply teacher choose to sleep?

I splashed my way down the corridor, checking behind me every few seconds for the teeth and hair I imagined could be flying towards my back. Rooms and doors began to whirl past. I remember passing a dozen doors, the music room, the drama centre, others that blurred into the beating of my heart and my panic. I only slowed when the end of the corridor was in sight. The staff room. The deputy head's office. School reception. And there, right next to the headmaster's office, was the room I'd been searching for.

SICK BAY. I felt as though the sign was lit up in neon and fireworks. "We made it, Kazu," I said, giving his head a little kiss.

She had to be here. Sleeping, and headless, behind this door. But what if I was wrong and the sick bay was empty? "Get a grip, Miku," I lectured myself. Because what if I was right?

Just then I heard an explosion of smashing glass from down the hall. At once the air filled with a supernatural scream. The nukekubi had made it inside the school.

I gulped. I grabbed the handle on the sick bay door, turning it oh so slowly, edging it around until I heard its inner mechanism click. The door was unlocked. I'd guessed it might be. Okuda wouldn't want to lock herself in, not without a head to think her way out again. So this was it. I gulped again, then turned the handle all the way, and opened the door.

Inside, the room was completely dark. The smell was overpowering, all the hospital smells I hate, disinfectant, bleach. But there was something else, a strange flowery smell.

Jasmine. Okuda's perfume.

I peeked around the door, but couldn't see a thing. Someone must have pulled the curtains shut across the back window. It was darker in this room than anywhere else in the school. I screwed up my eyes, squinting against the dark, and gradually, as my eyes adjusted, I began to see shapes, shadows. The cabinet along the right hand side. The chair on the left. And the bed, smack bang in the middle. I couldn't be sure, it might just be pillows, or a blanket laid strangely on the mattress, but it looked as if there was something on the bed. Something in the shape of a person. A body.

Had we found it? I needed to be sure.

Outside, a long way down the corridor, the head's undeathly scream echoed again. It seemed further away now, and I felt my skin tingle with relief. So far, so good.

I opened the door wider, creeping into the sick bay, trying not to breathe in its stink of jasmine and cleaning ammonia. It certainly looked like a body on the bed, but the part where the head should be was covered in darkest shadow. If I could get to the curtain, somehow let in some more light. Then we could be really sure.

I crept around on the left hand side, as far from the bed as I could get. If that was Mrs Okuda lying there, I didn't want her somehow to sense me. Who knew how these demons worked? She might not have her ears, but she still had the rest of her body.

I made it as far as the curtain, but as I pulled the blind aside several things happened all at once. First, a strange cold came over me, moving from the window to my hand and up my arm. I swear I could see ice crystals cracking and forming across my skin. As I moved the curtain aside I saw her, outside in the snow. The yuki-onna. And she was watching me.

She was tall, incredibly beautiful but pale as a ghost, and she was looking right at me, wearing a long white kimono, all alone outside in the snow. And in the next instant, she was gone, dissolved into a frosted mist. Just disappeared.

In that same instant, another blood-curdling

scream echoed through the school. It was the nukekubi, and it was getting closer.

I jumped away from the window. And I fell right back into the furniture, bumping a low table with a screech and knocking into a water jug. The jug teetered, then smashed to the floor in a cataclysm of noise, exploding into sheets of water and shards of glass. The body, for I could see it was a body now, sat bolt upright on the bed, its headless neck glowing in the crack of moonlight that shone from where I'd opened the curtain.

It was her, but I didn't wait to see what else she could do, head or no head.

I ran, rushing to the door of the sick bay, hardly checking the corridor before sprinting down and across the hall to another room. This one was a classroom, and empty by the look of it. I spun around, grabbing for a chair I could use to jam the door shut.

But the handle of the door started turning before I even got close.

"Takeshita-san..." came Mrs Okuda's sickly sweet voice. "I know you're in there."

I stepped backwards, away from the door and that awful voice. My whole body convulsed in fear, and I thought I might choke. But I still had Kazu. I couldn't just give up. I looked around for a weapon, some kind of broom or baseball bat I could use to smash her flying head. But there was nothing.

The door clicked open and began to swing inwards.

"Takeshita-san…"

I soon realised even a baseball bat wouldn't have helped. Mrs Okuda's purple painted fingernails curled around the wooden door seconds before her purple-lipped face appeared. The head had found the body. The nukekubi was whole.

"There you are," Okuda smiled, baring her teeth. A front tooth was chipped and her gum was bleeding. I guess smashing through a classroom window is difficult, even for a flying demon head.

She was still wearing her awful shiny caramel skirt and jacket, but her hair was loose, no longer wrapped around her head like a piece of fine art. And she'd forgotten to put her pearls back on. Her collar stood open, revealing the fiery red marks where her head had re-attached only moments earlier.

"And what have we here?" Okuda advanced slowly. "A baby, is it? No." She smiled, her eyes on Kazu and her teeth like an angry fox. "No, it's better than that. It's your brother, isn't it? Another Takeshita child. Shall I eat two in one day?"

"Get away from him," I warned, backing away.

She just laughed, an awful sound that grated inside my head. "Your Baba can't help you now, Takeshita-san."

I backed further away, thinking desperately. There had to be something I could do, some way to protect us. And then I remembered the cedar leaves. My jacket pocket was full of them.

I reached with my spare hand into my pocket, closing my fingers around the dry crispness of the leaves. At once I felt powerful. This should do it.

"Hah!" I shouted, flinging the handful of leaves right in Mrs Okuda's face.

But nothing happened. She just laughed again. "Those leaves might work against lesser demons," she sneered. "But I'm no amazake-baba, foolish child. Did your Baba teach you nothing? Do you even know what I am?"

I pulled Kazu closer and backed into another desk. "Stay away from us."

"Ah, but I've stayed away for so long already," Okuda crowed. "For hundreds of years I have hunted the Takeshitas, but always your Babas have protected you. And always that stupid child ghost has kept your family safe."

"Zashiko?" I echoed. Again? Baba had always

been careful to keep Zashiko happy in our house, leaving her toys and games and food, but had Zashiko really been so important?

"I don't know what you called your ghost." Okuda advanced slowly, pushing desks aside with a screeching slide. "But she's not here any more. You are alone now. You are far from that house, and your Baba is dead. Nothing can help you here."

I backed further away, bumping into something harder than a desk. The classroom wall. There was nowhere else to go.

"Give me the child," Okuda demanded, reaching for Kazu with two toffee-coloured arms. "Give me the child and perhaps I will let him live. Perhaps I will not be hungry for such a tiny morsel after I have finished with you."

The red marks around her neck grew angry, glowing like new scars. I watched in horror as they began to unwind, untying bits of her skin as they curled and uncurled in a line around her neck.

Chapter Twelve

I tried to scream for help, but my voice came out as tiny as a bird's. Instead I clutched Kazu closer to me and shook my head.

"Leave us alone."

"Leave you alone?" Okuda cackled. "When I have hunted the Takeshitas for so long? When I have followed you here across the oceans? Never! I will sup from the famous Takeshita blood, and then I will grow stronger than ever before. Your powers will transfer to me."

"But I don't have any powers…"

"No powers?" Okuda laughed again. "Your Baba and her Baba before that, all the Takeshita women have spiritual powers. Why do you think the child ghost stuck around for so many years? You are too young to know your powers, but not too young to share them with me. Now come, give me the boy."

The red marks around her neck wriggled as if worms were digging through her flesh. There was no way I was giving Kazu up, and never in a million years to her.

I screamed and dodged left, hoping to avoid her reaching arms. For a second it seemed to work, then her head came fully detached and she screamed even louder, zooming around the room in wild circles.

The scream slashed inside my brain, a katana sword ripping terror right through me. I dodged and ducked and ran, darting between desks in an attempt to get to the door. But Okuda's head kept between me and freedom, swooping back and forth like a black and hungry hawk. Her headless body just stood there, motionless and waiting, still as a statue.

"Give me the child!" the head screamed. **"Give me the child!"**

Fist-sized fireballs started dropping from the ceiling and the desklids began banging up and down by themselves. The purple-lipped head whipped up a wind, causing papers to whirl and jump in a frenzy. Even the curtains came to life, reaching for me in wild waves and banging against the glass of the window.

All I could think was to run. And I tried, dashing between desks, dodging fireballs, trying to steer clear of the head. Once it got so close that its black hair whipped my skin as it flew by in a rage.

But all at once I found myself back where I started, up against the wall, staring again at Okuda's headless body. And then, all too quickly, something grabbed me from behind.

I tried to fight but got nowhere. This thing seemed to have a dozen hands, to be made of rope itself. In seconds it had wrapped me up, coils of fabric holding me tight as an Egyptian mummy.

I struggled to get away, and then to cry out, but more fabric wrapped itself around my mouth, leaving only my nose free. I could hardly breathe as I twisted around, trying to see my attacker. But there was no one behind me - only the curtains, animated into evil life.

Panic growing, I watched Okuda's head fly back to her waiting body, the red marks swimming through her skin like living needles and thread, re-stitching body to head. At once the fireballs stopped falling and the desklids stopped banging. Everything was silent, but for her. In the distance I could hear a steady dripping. The water pipes. Perhaps we'd drown before she could eat us.

"Give me the child," she said, body reunited with head, arms reaching again for Kazu.

I struggled against the curtains, but I was

completely trapped. Only one arm was free, and that was the arm that held my brother. I couldn't fight her without dropping him.

I was beaten. I couldn't do anything to stop her. Tears began falling from my tired eyes. We'd been up all night, tackled a faceless demon, a flooded school, a shiny-skinned dragon woman, and all for nothing.

Okuda's purple-nailed hands curled around my sleeping brother, plucking him from my arm. I tried to fight her as soon as my arm was free, to punch her or rip my way out of the curtain prison. But it was hopeless. She was soon out of range of my punches, and the curtains didn't budge. I was totally trapped. And now she had Kazu.

"What a beautiful boy," the nukekubi sneered. "You must be very proud." She held him up, admiring him like a delicious doll. And for the first time that night, he woke up. He took one look at her and began to cry.

"Ugh," she said, wrinkling her nose in disgust. "Children. Who'd have one? Who'd be one?" She plonked Kazu on the teacher's desk and turned back to me, ignoring his wails.

I used my free arm to rip the curtain from my mouth. "It's OK, Kazu," I said, trying to sound comforting. "You'll be all right."

But Kazu looked at me, all tied up and trapped, and he cried even louder. He was right. There was no way things were going to be OK. I hoped like crazy he wouldn't have to watch me being eaten. And I hoped she might really let him go, after she'd finished with me.

Okuda advanced towards me, the red symbols on her neck working their way free. Her head was about to come off. She was licking her lips. I hoped I'd taste rotten, that she'd choke on my bones, that...

"Hey, fruit loop. Yeah you. You ever think about getting your hair done? 'Cos you look half-dead. You look awful. And you really need to do something about that problem with your neck."

My heart leapt. It was Cait!

She was poking her head round the classroom door. But what was she doing?

Run, I tried to scream. Run now, while you still have a chance. The sound died in my throat, the curtains crushing the air from my lungs.

But Cait didn't run. Instead she grinned and winked at me, as if this was some kind of game, just another of Alex's tricks on an unsuspecting supply teacher. And then she walked right into the classroom.

"That's got to be the worst suit I've ever seen,"

she said to Okuda, shaking her head in disgust. "It hurts my eyes just looking at it."

Okuda's body swung around. All her attention was now focused on Cait, but her head was still working its way free.

And still Cait didn't run.

"Hey, what you got there?" Cait chirped, looking at Kazu where he sat on the teacher's desk. He'd stopped screaming his lungs out, but the tears were still wet on his cheek and his little face was red. "I think that's Miku's baby brother. And I don't think he likes you. Why don't I just go and get him?"

Cait took a few steps towards Kazu. Distracted from her head-weaving, Okuda scurried to come between them.

"What's the matter, demon?" Cait asked. "Oh. What's that? You're going to need your arms if you want to keep me from grabbing Kazu? That's right. You better keep your head on while I'm in the room."

I had no idea what game Cait was playing. Once the head came off, Okuda could snap through Cait's neck and be back with her body in seconds, before Kazu had any chance of getting away. He was too young to walk, let alone escape.

"Foolish girl," Okuda spat, but her head stayed

close to her neck. Maybe Cait knew what she was doing. Okuda couldn't send her head flying around the room without leaving Kazu unprotected and alone with her headless body.

I couldn't hear what Cait said next. The sound of dripping water was getting louder, and her voice was drowned out by a steady gushing noise.

Okuda didn't seem to notice. She was riveted by Cait. Probably deciding what to do next. Attack and eat Cait now? Or grab Kazu first and eat Cait later? And I could do nothing to help. I was completely stuck, pinned down by the pinching, grabbing curtains.

The sound of running water was growing into a roar. I couldn't hear anything Cait and Okuda were saying.

Poor Kazu seemed lost and confused, all alone on the teacher's desk. He'd stopped crying, though, and began to show interest in what Cait was doing. He sat up and crawled a little way in her direction, closer to the edge of the desk.

Panicked, I tried to scream a warning, but the sound was trapped by the curtains before it could get out. Please stay still, Kazu, I willed. Don't move any further.

Cait and Okuda continued their face-off. Trickles of water began streaming through the open door.

CHAPTER THIRTEEN

Cait didn't seem to notice the growing tide. She was preparing to fight Okuda. The two of them moved in circles around the desks, like sumo wrestlers in the ring, each sizing the other up before their bout could begin. Except what could Cait do? She had no powers. No secret weapons. Nothing.

Suddenly Okuda swooped, but not at Cait. Instead she made a dash for the teacher's desk, grabbing Kazu and hoisting him high above her head in triumph. Her lips curled into a victory cry, but I heard nothing.

The sound of water was now so loud it was all I could hear. I couldn't even hear Kazu start screaming again, but I could tell from his face that he was yelling loud enough to bring the fire brigade. If only such a thing were possible. If only they would come.

With Kazu safe in her arms, Okuda seemed to think it was time for more action. She waved a hand and once again the desklids began banging and fireballs started dropping from the ceiling. The noise of desklids and waterfalls seemed to fill the entire room, a tsunami of sound.

But something strange was happening. Okuda's fireballs were fizzling out as soon as they hit the ground. She'd been so busy unravelling her head and preparing to fly that she hadn't noticed. While she'd been focused on Cait, the classroom had flooded. We were now ankle-deep in water.

Cait splashed across to where I stood trapped, taking care to stay clear of the waving, grabbing curtains. "Don't worry," she yelled over the noise. "She'll be here soon."

I had no idea what she was talking about, but then she pointed to the door.

There, unmistakably, was a series of growing ripples, each rushing to catch the other as they raced into the room. Something massive was behind those ripples, sweeping water into our room, surfing the waves up the corridor towards us.

Cait pointed again to the door and grinned. "She's coming."

The woman of the wet. The dragon woman.

She was back.

Okuda stared at the ripples, purple mouth hanging wide open. Slowly the desks stopped banging, the fireballs stopped falling. Even the curtains seemed to loosen their grip.

The nukekubi swung round to face the door, nearly losing her head in her haste. But she was still holding Kazu tightly.

What was she thinking? What were those red markings doing as the dragon woman approached? Sewing Okuda together? Or unravelling?

Suddenly the rushing of water was gone. Even Kazu seemed to sense that something was happening. His screams became a quiet whimper. Something large was sliding, swishing, slithering its way towards us. I nearly cheered.

The dragon woman was coming.

As soon as her snake-like body appeared in the corridor, Okuda gasped and stepped backwards, away from the door. "Nure-onna."

Then everything fell silent.

"Nukekubi," the green woman hissed. "I see you have the child."

"And what of it?" Okuda sneered, holding Kazu closer.

"What are you doing so far from home?"

the dragon woman asked, almost sadly. "Must you insist on hunting these children?" She stayed in the doorway, her red tongue forked and ready.

Okuda growled, baring her teeth like a fox. "But you are also far from home, woman of the wet. This is not your place."

The nure-onna slid further into the room, revealing more of her scaly green skin. "But there you are wrong, nukekubi," she said, smiling so that her fangs shone and glittered in the light.

"What?" Okuda spat. "This is not our country, nure-onna. You have no power over me here."

But I could sense Okuda's confidence dropping. Was she scared of the dragon woman? Bit by bit, the curtains were loosening their grip. Careful not to draw too much attention, I wrestled my other arm free and began to unwrap myself.

The two demons didn't seem to notice.

The dragon woman flicked her tongue and raised one perfect eyebrow at Okuda. "Where one belongs," she hissed, "depends on one's actions…"

"Don't be stupid," Okuda snarled. "Your kind don't belong here."

"No," the nure-onna hissed. "It is you who is not welcome here, nukekubi. I came tonight on the bidding of the Takeshita zashiki-warashi, the child ghost, Zashiko. I came to hunt you, with this child as your bait."

The dragon woman pointed at Kazu and I gasped. Bait? She was no better than Okuda. It didn't seem to matter who won this contest. Either way, we were doomed.

"But," the dragon woman continued, gesturing at Cait and me, "these children took him and deserved him, and with that they bought your life, for one more night."

"What are you talking about?" Okuda sneered.

"I have returned because this curly-haired child asked for my help." The dragon woman's eyes flashed and she nodded her hissing head at Cait.

Cait blushed. "Turns out she's OK after all," she whispered, pulling aside bits of curtain to help me escape.

But could the nure-onna really be OK? I couldn't forget what she'd just said. She'd brought Kazu as bait? Human bait? What kind of demon was she?

Cait and I both stared at the nure-onna, whose snaking body rippled with muscle as she slid further into the room.

Okuda backed away, still holding Kazu.

"I came here today to eat these children. And that is my right."

"And that," hissed the dragon woman, "is your downfall, nukekubi. For you will be judged by your actions."

Okuda held Kazu close to her open mouth, threatening. "Don't come any closer."

"I don't need to," the nure-onna said. "Your home is not here, nukekubi."

For a second Okuda was silent, then something strange happened. Her face seemed to grow purple, just like her awful lipstick.

"What are you doing?" she gasped. "What's happening?"

"You are being judged." The dragon woman did nothing, just stared at Okuda's flushing face, her red eyes narrow as slits.

I pulled free from the last of the curtains, watching in awe.

"But he's so heavy," Okuda gasped, confused. "He's just a baby. It's not possible for him to be this... heavy..." Her face was glowing red with effort now. Sweat was pouring from her brow and her arms began shuddering, as if carrying an extraordinary weight.

"It's Kazu," I whispered to Cait. "She did it to me earlier."

I watched as Okuda's entire body shook with the effort of carrying my tiny brother.

Suddenly the dragon woman reared up on her snake's body. "You care for this child?" she demanded, addressing Okuda as the nukekubi struggled to hang on to Kazu's weight.

"Of course not," Okuda spat. "You know I don't, so don't bother asking. And stop what it is that you're doing." She was trying to fling Kazu away, but her arms had stopped responding.

The dragon demon hissed again, her eyes blood-red and angry. "You promise to take good care of this child?" she asked, spitting each word from between dripping white fangs.

"Rubbish…" Okuda gasped. "Never. Why are you doing this?" She staggered to one knee, as if crushed under a massive load.

"This," roared the dragon woman, "is my work. My place. My home. And Zashiko's plan. And if you will not care for this child…"

"I…will…not…" Okuda struggled for breath, falling now on both knees, as if she was praying for forgiveness.

"If you will not care for this child," the nure-onna continued, "then you choose your own fate." Her tongue flicked again and again, and her eyes began to bulge inside her green face.

For an instant it seemed that Okuda might be

strong enough to stand again, but that moment passed. She wailed where she knelt on the floor, a wrenching noise that sent Kazu once again into a flood of tears.

The angry red characters around Okuda's neck were lost in the rush of blood to her head, but I could see them still working away, stitching or unstitching to set her head free.

Just as her body collapsed to the ground, Okuda's head flew up, cackling and wailing.

"You cannot beat me," the head crowed, sweeping in a wide circle above our heads.

"I am sorry, nukekubi," said the dragon woman. "But I already have." She turned to stare at the place where Okuda's body had been, but all that was left was a shrinking pile of caramel clothes.

Okuda's body was literally shrivelling away, disappearing. She was being crushed into nothing.

"No…" Okuda's head gave one final shriek, then fell limp and lifeless to the floor, its black hair flung out on the ground like a flag.

Everyone was silent for a long time.

"Is she…?" Cait asked eventually.

The woman of the wet nodded slowly. "It was Zashiko's plan. And my work."

"When the body is destroyed…" Cait whispered.

"…the nukekubi is dead," I finished, wondering

130

at what we had just seen. Then I shook my head to clear my thoughts. We were forgetting one important thing.

I rushed across the classroom to the pile of clothes that had been Mrs Okuda. There, sitting happily, though his cheeks were still wet, was my brother.

"Kazu," I cried, scooping him up in my arms. He smiled and gurgled a hello. He seemed fine, and he weighed just the same as ever. "What happened here?" I asked, confronting the dragon woman again. "Who are you?"

"I have already told you," she said. "I am the nure-onna. Woman of the wet." Her tongue slid slowly in and out, like a snake resting after a large meal. "I do not usually travel so far from Japan, but this nukekubi was causing trouble, and the Takeshitas are well known in my circles. It seems Zashiko still cares for you," she smiled. "All the way from Japan, she still watches for you."

"What about you?" Cait asked. "Now what?"

The serpent demon hissed, a soft, sighing sound. "I think I like it here. There is plenty for me to do."

"You know you can't always flood our school," Cait grinned. "And not all our teachers are cut-throat demons."

The dragon woman smiled. "I know. Maybe you

131

will not need to see me again. There are others who have followed you, the noppera-bō, the ōkubi, the amazake-baba and more. Most will not cause you trouble. They are just curious. You are Takeshita, after all. You carry your grandmother's blood, and her grandmother's blood before that. The nukekubi was right. You have great powers, though you do not know it yet." The demon looked distressed. A strange trickling noise had interrupted her thoughts. "I must go," she said. "The waters recede."

She reversed her massive body out of the door, riding slowly on the retreating waves.

"But, what kind of powers?" I asked, desperate to know more before she left.

She smiled at me, fangs gleaming. "You will find them. Already you have discovered more than I thought possible. And your curly-haired friend is a wise one, and brave." She turned and nodded kindly at Cait. "Together, you will discover even more."

There was a strange gurgling sound, like water draining from a sink, and then, in an instant, she had gone.

I rushed to the door and peered down the corridor. But all I could see was the gleam of drying puddles. The woman of the wet had disappeared.

CHAPTER FOURTEEN

We didn't have long to wait till morning. The sun was already climbing the sky as we jumped from our classroom window, passing Kazu like a delicate treasure between us. All around, the snow was melting, turning into tiny streams and trickles down the street. I wondered about the yuki-onna. Where had she disappeared to?

"Wonder if there'll be any school today," Cait said, kicking at the snow as we walked home.

I grimaced. "There'd better not be a maths test. I don't think I could get a single question right. I'm exhausted."

So, it seemed, was Kazu. He was asleep again, breathing soundly in Cait's arms with not a sign of the cough that had troubled him before.

"Hey, Miku Mouse," a voice yelled from down the street.

I turned to see who it was, just in time to get a snowball in the face. Choking and spluttering, I cleared the icy snow from my eyes, desperate to see what demon was attacking us this time.

"How's your mum?" the demon yelled. Except it wasn't a demon. It was Alex, grinning and scooping more snow for another attack. "Did you hear? No school today. The pipes burst and the whole place flooded overnight. Cool, huh?"

Another snowball came sailing across the street in our direction.

We ducked and I gathered some snow for a counter-attack. "My mum's in hospital actually," I said. "She hurt her ankle on the ice last night." I hurled the snowball in Alex's direction and started walking away. "Come on, Cait, let's get home."

I expected a snowball in the back at any moment, but none came.

"Sorry about your mum," Alex called. There was a pause, but I didn't look back. "Will we see you at the park later on?" he yelled.

This time I turned around, not sure if Alex was teasing or not.

His face seemed serious.

"Maybe," I called, and he smiled.

"Cool. You can come too, O'Neill. We're planning

134

a mega snowfight. Awesome." He hurled another snowball at us and we scurried away.

"You really going to a snowfight with Alex?" Cait asked.

"Dunno." I grinned. "Depends on whether Mum's OK. And whether Mrs Williams can babysit Kazu."

I let us through my front door and we floated like sleepwalkers into the flat.

"Hey, you want to stay over tonight as well?" I asked, grinning.

"Will it be like last night?" Cait asked.

"Maybe."

"Then maybe," Cait answered, grinning back. "But first, we eat. I'm starving. We'll need our strength if we're going to throw snowballs all afternoon."

We tucked Kazu into his cot and cranked out another pizza, this time Hawaiian.

While it was cooking, I dragged a chair over to our front door and stuck another cedar leaf in the door-frame. Better safe than sorry, even if they did only work on minor demons.

And although we also ate this pizza fast enough to burn our tongues, we left a spare piece on the bench, just in case Zashiko was passing by and in the mood for something new. I hoped my Baba would be proud.

I still prefer teddy bears and bunny rabbits to ghosts and evil spirits, but it's too late for that now. One day I'll tell Kazu all about what happened, and I'll teach him more about the Takeshita ghosts and demons that still haunt us. Who knows what could be waiting just around the corner?

If you ever come up against a nukekubi of your own, I hope that some of what you've read here will help you. Don't forget what you've learned, and keep your eyes peeled for strange red markings or peculiar itchings. And if you wake up one morning to find that your pillow is down by your feet instead of up by your head, or the light in your ceiling is rocking like a boat, be very thankful. It could be that someone is looking out for you.

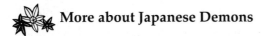 **More about Japanese Demons**

Better known as *yokai* (妖怪), supernatural demons have
featured in Japanese fairy tales and folklore for centuries.
Many hundreds of *yokai* exist: some came originally from
China while others sprang up to explain spooky stories or
strange happenings. Scholars have been cataloguing *yokai*
species in encyclopedias and databases since the 1770s.

Yokai are still popular in modern Japan: they have
restaurant dishes named after them, statues sold of them,
books written about them. They star in manga comics and
movies, are used to advertise banks and beer, and might
still be blamed when something strange goes bump in the
night.

The Japanese characters used to write *yokai* mean
"bewitching" and "suspicious", and the word can refer to
all kinds of supernatural spirits: goblins, ghosts, monsters
and more. *Yokai* can be bringers of luck or harbingers of
doom, clippers of hair or shakers of beans. They can be
good, evil, or just plain strange.

Only one thing is certain about *yokai*: one is probably
watching you right now!

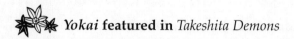 *Yokai* **featured in** *Takeshita Demons*

Amazake baba (**Sweet sake woman**) 甘酒婆

This *yokai* takes the shape of an old woman with a gentle voice, but don't be fooled. If you answer the door when she knocks, chances are you'll fall ill with chicken pox.

Ittan momen (**Animated cotton**) 一反木綿

Ittan momen are long bits of cloth that can come to life in the night. They love to tangle around your body and might even try to suffocate you, so keep an eye on your curtains.

Noppera-bō (**Faceless ghost**) のっぺら坊

Is the person sitting next to you really who you think they are? *Noppera-bō* are experts at pretending to be other people, and they love to cause trouble. Just when you least expect it their features can disappear, melting away to leave their face as empty as a blank page.

Nukekubi (**Cut-throat**) 抜首

During the day you might mistake this *yokai* for a normal person, but be warned. At night, while its body is sleeping, its head can detach and fly around hunting for delicious things to eat (like children and puppy dogs).

Nure-onna (**Woman of the wet**) 濡女

With the torso of a woman and the body of a snake, this fearsome *yokai* has wicked claws and a long forked tongue She's strong enough to crush a tree in the coils of her massive tail.

O-kubi (**Big throat**) 大首

If you're ever staring up at the sky and spot an enormous head in the clouds, watch out! Spotting an *o-kubi* usually means something awful is just around the corner…

Sakabashira (**Inverted pillar**) 逆柱

Did it happen by mistake? Or did someone do it on purpose? Whatever the reason, if some part of your house was built upside-down, your entire house is doomed to be haunted.

Yuki-onna (**Snow woman**) 雪女

Tall, pale and icily beautiful, this *yokai* is a spirit of the snow. She leaves no footprints, preferring to float above the ground, and she can disappear in a puff of cold mist.

Zashiki-warashi (**House ghost**) 座敷童

This mischievous *yokai* haunts houses and usually appears in the shape of a child. If your house is haunted by a *zashiki-warashi*, count yourself lucky, but don't forget to take good care of it. If your house ghost ever chooses to leave you, your luck will quickly end.

Turn the page for an exclusive preview
of the first chapter of

TAKESHITA DEMONS
THE FILTH LICKER

another demon adventure for Miku and Cait.

CHAPTER ONE

"Cait, are you still there?" I could hear breathing on the other end of the phone, but Cait's voice had disappeared, cut off halfway through a sentence. "Hello?"

It was dark outside, late on the night before School Camp, and I had a bad feeling in my gut that was cutting like knives. I was supposed to be packing shirts and shoes and lucky charms to take to camp, but I hadn't even opened my case.

The phone crackled. "Sorry," Cait whispered. "I had to go quiet. I'm s'posed to be in bed. Dad'll freak if he finds me up this late."

So she was still there. Still OK. Relief prickled down my arms.

"What's up?" she asked. "Why are you calling so late?"

I swallowed. "It's about camp," I began. "I've got this feeling..."

Cait didn't hesitate. "I know," she said. "Me too."

I grinned despite the churning in my belly. Of course Cait would understand. She'd been with me through everything, helping me break into our school and rescue my brother, making friends with a half-dragon water-woman, even standing up to Mrs Okuda after she'd become a child-eating nukekubi demon. Since the night we'd met the demons, Cait and I had been virtually inseparable. Unlike Mrs Okuda and her head.

"I've been doing a lot of thinking," Cait continued. "About camp. I think we're going to need a few extra things...."

I listened, on the edge of my bed.

"But it's hard to know," she said. "I think I'll take two, then I can wear one at dinner or whatever, and have the other if Mr Lloyd makes us go hiking. Are you taking two? Or maybe we should go for three?"

"What? What are you talking about?"

The phone went silent. "Jeans," Cait said. "What are you talking about?"

"Demons." I hissed the word into the phone, as if a demon might be listening outside my door right that very second. "At camp."

The phone stayed silent.

"Cait?" What was going on over there? Maybe she wasn't safe after all…

To keep in touch with Miku and Cait and find out more about *Takeshita Demons: The Filth Licker* visit **www.franceslincoln.com/takeshitademons** or email **takeshitademons@frances-lincoln.com**

TAKESHITA DEMONS

is the winner of the inaugural 2009
Frances Lincoln Diverse Voices
Children's Book Award

The Frances Lincoln Diverse Voices Children's Book Award was founded jointly by Frances Lincoln Limited and Seven Stories, in memory of Frances Lincoln (1945-2001) to encourage and promote diversity in children's fiction.

The Award is for a manuscript that celebrates cultural diversity in the widest possible sense, either in terms of its story or the ethnic and cultural origins of its author.

The prize of £1500, plus the option for Frances Lincoln Children's Books to publish the novel, is awarded to the best work of unpublished fiction for 8-12-year-olds by a writer aged 16 years or over, who has not previously published a novel for children. The winner of the Award is chosen by an independent panel of judges.

Please see the Frances Lincoln or Seven Stories website for further details.

www.franceslincoln.com
www.sevenstories.org.uk

The running and administration of the Frances Lincoln Diverse Voices Children's Book Award is led by Seven Stories, in Newcastle upon Tyne. Seven Stories is Britain's children's literature museum. It brings the wonderful world of children's books to life through lively exhibitions and inspiring learning and events programmes. Seven Stories is saving Britain's children's literature by building a unique archive that shows how authors and illustrators turn their thoughts and ideas into finished books of stories, poems and pictures.

Seven Stories believes that children should be able to choose books that reflect the lives of children from different cultures in the world today. Frances Lincoln, in whose memory the Award was founded, had an unswerving commitment to finding talented writers who brought new voices, characters, places and plots to children's books.

Arts & Business

Frances Lincoln Limited and Seven Stories gratefully acknowledge the support of Arts & Business for the Frances Lincoln Diverse Voices Children's Book Award.

CRISTY BURNE

has joint New Zealand and Australian
citizenship, has travelled widely and
lived for several years in Japan as a teacher
and editor. It was during this time that she
became fascinated with Japanese folklore and
the supernatural *yokai* - demons - which are very
much a part of Japanese culture, but little known
outside Japan. Cristy has spent most of her career
as a science writer, and currently works for a
computing network designed to solve global problems.
She won a Young and Emerging Writer fellowship
with Varuna House, in the Blue Mountains,
Australia, and *Takeshita Demons* is her first
published book. Cristy and her family
live in Perth, Western Australia.